Badger, Boomer and Bathroom Bob

Badger, Boomer and Bathroom Bob

John Wilson

Copyright © 2013 John Wilson

The moral right of the author has been asserted.

Apart from any fair dealing for the purposes of research or private study,
or criticism or review, as permitted under the Copyright, Designs and Patents
Act 1988, this publication may only be reproduced, stored or transmitted, in
any form or by any means, with the prior permission in writing of the
publishers, or in the case of reprographic reproduction in accordance with
the terms of licences issued by the Copyright Licensing Agency. Enquiries
concerning reproduction outside those terms should be sent to the publishers.

Matador
9 Priory Business Park,
Wistow Road, Kibworth Beauchamp,
Leicestershire. LE8 0RX
Tel: (+44) 116 279 2299
Fax: (+44) 116 279 2277
Email: books@troubador.co.uk
Web: www.troubador.co.uk/matador

ISBN 978 1780884 035

British Library Cataloguing in Publication Data.
A catalogue record for this book is available from the British Library.

Typeset by Troubador Publishing Ltd, Leicester, UK
Printed and bound in Great Britain by
Clays Ltd, St Ives plc

Matador is an imprint of Troubador Publishing Ltd

*To Jack Carter
who kept urging me to write –
and who believes an ounce of
bourbon is worth a pound of
almost anything else*

Contents

Trouble Begins   1
   1   A Close Call   3

Two Days Later   9
   2   A Bad Day   11
   3   The Dean Greets a Visitor   17
   4   A Revelation and a Warning   25
   5   An Unexpected Discovery   38
   6   Lieutenant McCallister   43

Late Winter into Early Spring: More Trouble from Every Quarter   51
   7   The Plotters   53
   8   Janet Harbrough   64
   9   Zo Talks Tough   70
  10   Prigley Stirs the Pot   77

New Developments   93
  11   The Meeting   95
  12   Some Action Taken   113
  13   Another Meeting   120
  14   Featherheft   126
  15   The First Letter   132
  16   The Plotters Meet Again   141

Charlie — 147
17 Reconnaissance — 149
18 Charlie — 157

Near the End of a Difficult School Year — 163
19 Ruth Reports — 165
20 The Second Letter — 171
21 The Outing — 175
22 The Third Letter — 191

Halcyon Days in June — 201
23 The Graduation — 203
24 A Final Communication — 218

Summertime — 227
25 Bathroom Bob Sounds a Sour Note — 229
26 A Final Revelation — 236

Epilogue — 245

Trouble Begins

Chapter One

A Close Call

From the outside, only one light was visible on the third floor of the law school. It cast its feeble glow into the darkness and onto the bare, upper branches of nearby trees. The dean was working late, and the illumination came from a standing lamp near the window of his office and, less directly, from the green shaded lamp on his desk.

Normally, the dean did not work in solitude into the evening hours, but he was perplexed, indeed alarmed, by a problem he had encountered that afternoon. Seated at his desk in shirt sleeves, tie askew, he was scribbling figures on a yellow pad, then vigorously erasing them with angry, jerky movements and scribbling again.

A second light blinked on, this time on the second floor where faculty offices and a mailroom were located. It was not unusual for a member of the faculty to work late, perhaps preparing for a difficult class the next day, but the brightness of this light was sporadic – at once a strong gleam, then very dim – as if someone was swinging a flashlight from side to side.

All was still, a soft quiet as if the predicted snow was already falling. An occasional blare of a car horn interrupted the silence, but that was all. And then there was a muffled shout – or perhaps a barely audible scream? Hearing it, the dean sat upright, listening intently, but where had it come from? There was no further sound.

Puzzled and uncertain what to do, the dean rose and walked to the doorway of his office. He could hear noises within the building more easily in the corridor, and it was there, still listening intently, that he heard a shriek followed – he was nearly certain – by "No, no, get away from me," in a rising crescendo of terror. He decided quickly that the sound had come from the floor below, and he dashed to the stairs at the end of the corridor.

"I'm coming, I'm coming," he shouted as he pounded down the stairs.

When he reached the landing to the second floor, he met Henry, a short, pudgy librarian who emerged at the same time from the floor below. Henry had presumed he was the only person on duty that evening, and he looked relieved to see the dean. "It came from in here, I think," he said, holding the door open from the stairwell to the second floor.

The dean ran inside. There, in a dimly lit hallway, he found a young woman leaning against the wall outside the mailroom. Aside from a flickering, fluorescent light near the stairwell, the corridor and its offices were dark. In the muted light, the dean could see that she was a short, pretty woman and that she was breathing in convulsive gasps. "I'm so glad someone was here," she said haltingly. "Thank goodness you came when you did."

"Are you all right?" the dean shouted, his voice far too loud under the circumstances.

She nodded her head slowly in affirmation.

"What happened?"

Henry was standing behind the dean, open-mouthed, glancing around nervously.

For several moments, the young woman said nothing.

Then, with a quivering finger, she pointed at a nearby office with its door slightly ajar. She said: "He came from there."

"He? Who?"

"A man... a man, and he was coming toward me when I screamed. He... I'm sure, he was going to rape me, or hurt me, but then he heard you and ran down the stairs."

"What stairs? We were on the stairs."

"The internal stairs. Over there." She pointed toward a barely visible doorway at the far end of the hall.

"How would he have known that...?" The dean stopped speaking, perplexed. "Henry," he said, turning slightly, "go and check to see if anyone's there. Hurry!"

Henry stood rooted in place, his eyes wide.

"I said 'hurry!' He may still be there."

Henry sidled around the dean and began walking slowly down the corridor with frequent backward glances. "Is there a light?" he said in a quavering voice.

The dean retraced his steps to the corridor's entrance and, finding a switch, snapped on overhead lights. He returned to the young woman.

"Any idea who it was?"

"No," she faltered, starting to cry.

"It's all right... you're all right now."

He heard Henry shout from the end of the hallway. "There's no one here."

"Okay, thanks for looking." The dean turned again to the young woman, a frown on his features. "I don't mean to upset you, but I need to know who you are and why you're here. This is a law school, and I'm Dean Ansari."

"I know who you are," she sniffled. "I'm a new employee in the Career Services Office. My name is Alice Hodges. You haven't met me, but the director pointed you out to me yesterday."

"And why you're...?"

"And?... Oh, yes, I was driving by after seeing a girlfriend, and I remembered I'd made a mistake in a letter to an employer – a pretty big firm, so it was important. I wanted to correct it before it was sent out, so I thought I'd retrieve it before the mail was picked up in the morning."

"That was very conscientious of you," the dean said, nodding his head approvingly. "So, you came in for a letter. And you were here in this hallway on the way to the mailroom, or maybe coming from the mailroom, when something happened. Am I correct?"

"Yes, I was going to the mailroom," Alice said slowly, unwilling or unready to relive the experience.

The dean could see how beautiful and fragile she appeared in the glare of the overhead lights. He spoke to Henry, who by this time had returned. "Turn down some of those lights, if you can, and let's find out what happened without this looking like the third degree."

Henry quickly complied, and Alice resumed talking. "I was walking to the mailroom, like I said, when I saw this figure – his clothes all dark – come out of that office over there." She pointed again to a nearby door. "He stopped and stared at me, and that's when I screamed. I noticed he was, like, wearing some kind of mask, like maybe a stocking, pulled over his head. And he had a piece of paper in his hand. It... it seemed like the longest time we just stood there, looking at each other. I was really scared. Then he started toward me, and I... I screamed again, and, I think, yes, I told him to get away from me.

Then I heard you on the stairs, and he did too. I guess he

didn't know anyone else was near. He just walked past me and said something like… like 'your lucky night, bitch,' and he ran down the corridor before you and this man appeared."

Alice started to sniffle again, and the dean handed her his clean handkerchief. "I'm sure he frightened you badly," he said, "but you're all right. You should go home, get some rest, and take tomorrow off."

"Oh, no," Alice said, looking up at him, her large eyes red with tears. "I'll be okay. But thank you."

The dean spoke to Henry. "Why don't you retrieve that letter and then walk her to her car, if you don't mind, and see that she's safely off. I'm going back to my office. Please meet me there as soon as you can."

* * * * *

His task completed, Henry appeared at the dean's office door a few minutes later. The dean had placed the materials from his desk inside a cabinet and was seated in a chair by a coffee table at one end of the room. He waved Henry to a couch on the other side of the table.

"That may have been a close call," he said.

Henry nodded.

"But in the end, no harm done," the dean continued with a piercing glance. "While, of course, you must do what you think best, I'd appreciate it if you wouldn't say anything about this to anyone. I'll speak to Alice in the morning and ask her to do the same."

Henry looked troubled. "You mean, no report to the police?"

"I'll call them in the morning about an unauthorized entry after we've checked to see if anything was stolen."

Henry's brow furrowed. "Even if it wasn't a rape, wasn't it an assault? What about her role in this incident? Don't you think... ?"

The dean interrupted him. "Most likely it was just a trespass and maybe burglary, and possibly he stole something. We'll find out. But nothing happened to her. He didn't molest her or say he was going to. In fact, if her recollection is correct, he said it was her lucky night when he walked past her. All he did was stand near a doorway and then run to a stairwell."

"She was terribly frightened," Henry countered with gathering conviction. "Think of the circumstances. It was dark, she was alone, and she thought he was going to assault her, maybe even rape her. People should be warned."

"Warned about what? If people get frightened by someone standing still and then walking toward them, we could all be criminals. As I said," the dean repeated emphatically, "for the good of the school, I'd appreciate it if you wouldn't discuss this with anyone. We can't afford bad publicity."

Two Days Later

Chapter Two

A Bad Day

The dean arrived early for work the next morning. He was perplexed. How could the intruder have gained entry to the office when faculty members lock their doors in the evening before leaving? And how did the intruder know the location of the internal staircase? Was he – or she – a student or a member of the staff who had somehow acquired a copy of the key to that particular office? The voice had apparently been masculine, but it could have been faked. It was too bad, due to dim lighting, that Alice could not provide a better description.

Using his master key, the dean entered the office from which the intruder had emerged and looked around. Nothing of value seemed to have been taken. A calculator and expensive clock had not been touched. He left a note asking the professor whose office it was to check to determine if anything valuable was missing and then report back to him.

Dean Ansari then returned to his office and called Alice Hodges. In a sleepy voice, she answered the phone. "Yes," she said, "I'm all right," and while she appreciated the dean's concern, she planned to come to work by mid morning. Upon being questioned, she added that she was sure from his physical appearance and tone of voice that the intruder was a male.

Later that morning, having satisfied himself that nothing had been stolen, the dean reported the incident to the police. The desk sergeant was polite but not concerned and said vaguely that someone might come by the school and talk to him. It seemed that a mere unauthorized entry into an office was very low on a scale of importance, and in fact no one from the police department showed up until other events intervened.

Several important matters occupied the dean for the remainder of the day, so that he was unable to get back to the problem that had so worried him on the preceding night. Finally, after his first appointment the following day, he removed the papers on which he had been working from a file cabinet and examined them again. Seated behind his desk, he was occupied with this task for most of the morning. The radiator was clanking in the corner, and he had kept his jacket on – a brown, herringbone tweed with patches on the elbows – instead of hanging it on the wooden clothes tree by the door. It was still chilly in his office, but he hardly noticed. His focus was on an office calculator at one side of his desk on which he had been tabulating numbers from a file folder in his lap with the label "Financial Aid" written carefully, in block letters, across the top.

He had studied every paper in the folder, as he had the documents in other file folders scattered across his desk, some dog-eared from use and two or three designated Annual Budget by academic year.

Holding the tips of his fingers against his eyes, he pressed them inward. Even though he had checked the figures every way he could imagine to detect an error in his calculations, there seemed little doubt that money was missing. Lots of it, although the trail was difficult to follow. Copies of letters to student aid recipients were in the files, each with a designated award of a grant or a loan, and no student had complained that the money had not been forthcoming. Adding up the awards offered in the letters for the past couple of academic years had been time-consuming; that task completed, the total was less than the amount budgeted or the amount that had presumably been spent. In each year, the difference was about $75,000.

Out of a total financial aid budget of several hundred thousand dollars, no one had detected the difference. Neither the budget director nor the dean had done the internal arithmetic.

Indeed, were it not for drastically declining applications for admission in the previous three years, resulting in a corresponding decline in enrollments, an audit would never have been performed. But the law school's financial situation had become precarious, and so he had asked his staff for a careful review of the money expended in every department. The financial aid totals revealed a discrepancy. When this was brought to his attention, he thought there must have been an innocent mistake or some legitimate, improperly recorded payment. The file folders' contents, unfortunately, did not reveal it. In fact, they only revealed expenditures in aggregate amounts every month, without specifying the awards per recipient, and the totals marched inexorably to the erroneous, year-end conclusion that the budget was in balance.

The dean removed the file folder from his lap and jerked it violently up and down as if to shake loose an answer. In disgust, he hurled it back on his desk, then riffled rapidly and aimlessly through several of the other folders, dropping them one by one in a scattered heap on top of the first. Slowly, he spun his chair around and stared at the grayness outside the window. With his hands folded behind his head and his jaw working back and forth, as it always did whenever he was angry or excited, he sat immobile for several minutes.

Why, he mused, is every problem the one you least expect, and why, as one difficulty is resolved, does another inevitably take its place, as if administration abhors a vacuum? His vexed thoughts wandered to another, unanticipated problem, only tangentially related to the matter at hand but equally worrisome in terms of its impact on the reputation of the school. On the same evening that the intruder had so frightened Alice Hodges, a male student, Thomas Headly, had apparently tripped and fallen to his death through his apartment's fourth floor living room window. A local newspaper reported that just before his death he had been carousing at a loud student party in the same building to which the police had been called, and he had lost his balance in an inebriated condition. The paper also mentioned that he was despondent about his grades. The dean remembered him, however, as an excellent student, and while the deportment of students off campus was usually of little concern to school authorities, Thomas seemed an unlikely candidate for an alcoholic binge.

Of immediate importance, Thomas had worked as a part-time employee in the university's Accounting Office and hence he was the first person to whom the dean would have directed an inquiry about the financial aid shortfall. Now any questions would have to be directed to Thomas' superior: a large, forbidding female, Allison Fetherheft, who, as Vice President for Administration and Provost, had mastered irritation, brevity and obfuscation in equal measure. Once Ms. Fetherheft had been dean of students, and the students had referred to her as Dean Dreadnought. No longer in use, the nickname was apt. It made the dean's stomach groan.

* * * * *

The office in which he was sitting was overly pretentious for a second-rate law school rapidly becoming third-rate, but it was comfortable. It was like the library or reading room in a Victorian mansion. The walls had oak wainscoting, and at one end was a plump leather sofa behind a long, oak coffee table. At the opposite end, farthest from the door, was the dean's solid desk, now covered with folders. Broad, made also of oak, it had a banker's reading lamp with a rounded, green shade on one side. There was a wooden chair next to the desk where Mrs. Ackerman, the dean's secretary, usually sat. Four other chairs were scattered near the couch and coffee table.

The principal denizen of this lair matched his surroundings. His thinning hair was mottled brown with flecks of white. Tall and slightly stooped, with an oval face characterized by an aquiline nose, he had soft, dark eyes that crinkled with ready laughter and a toothy smile. His name was Massoud Ansari, the only person of Iranian descent on the faculty. His father had been a prominent economist in the years before the downfall of the Shah. He had escaped with his family to England and then to the United States when the dean was a small boy.

Most of the students and, behind his back, the staff and faculty, referred to him as Badger. The name's origin was obscure but probably originated from his persistent manner of questioning in class and his penchant for the color brown. Once elevated to an administrative position, the name had fallen into partial disuse. Other members of the faculty also had pet names conferred by students over time to highlight their personal characteristics.

It was snowing, which did not improve the dean's mood. He kept thinking what a terrible mistake he had made when he left a tenured professorship at a good law school to become dean of this God-forsaken place. He thought: eighteen years out of Yale Law School and this is what I have to show for a career? Everyone blames the declining enrollments on me, when it's the damn faculty's fault for not maintaining our reputation by imposing strict academic standards. Not for the first time, he berated himself: I'm too gentle, sometimes befuddled, and I wasn't cut out to be a disciplinarian and a cheerleader at the same time. And now this mess.

Wallowing in self pity was not the dean's style, and he soon switched his thinking to remedial action. It seemed he should at least convene an emergency meeting of the Financial Aid Committee, which consisted of two students, Ruth Dinsmore and Kevin Pannelli, and three members of the faculty. They might suggest leads, although he was not sanguine that much practical help would be forthcoming.

With this thought in mind, he decided to descend one flight to the faculty floor and consult immediately with the faculty members of the committee. However, his knocks on their doors went unanswered, and he retreated to his office where he instructed Mrs. Ackerman to arrange a meeting with them as soon as possible. His secretary then reminded him that a visitor was scheduled to arrive in about ten minutes.

Just what I need, he thought, some damn fool interruption.

Chapter Three

The Dean Greets a Visitor

Massoud Ansari was dean of Crabshaw School of the Law. Students and alumni were known in the community as Crabbies. It was a medium-sized, private law school in a medium-sized city in a medium-sized state in the middle of the country. It was the epitome of average. Asked about its salient characteristics, the Admissions Director usually fell silent; sometimes she would fumble for a moment and then declare: "We train people for the law." Now and then she would add: "We have the advantage of being located between Harrisburg, Pennsylvania, and Sacramento, California." She never explained what that advantage might be, and one applicant, to her considerable mortification, had the temerity to snicker.

The Admissions Director might have said, but never did, that of the approximately two hundred law schools in the country approved by the American Bar Association, Crabshaw – to her knowledge – was the only one with an alma mater. It began with the memorable words: "Oh Crabshaw, my Crabshaw." Played to a martial air, it contained verses such as:

> We long to be among that retinue
> Who have mastered trover, debt and detinue
> and
> Upon that noble brow, thy name
> Is burnished by thy graduates' fame.

A wealthy alumnus had composed the song. His fame, which had a restricted radius, was built upon winning personal injury law suits. Eager to obtain a bequest, the school had adopted his musical effort, and every member of the faculty had been asked to memorize the words and sing them in unison at graduation. Compliance had been disappointing. When the alumnus died, he left his entire fortune to the state university.

On this particular morning – two days after the incident outside the mail room – snow had been drifting down since late in the preceding afternoon. Crabshaw School of the Law occupied an old, brownstone building with tall, multi-paned windows in ornate casements, and snow had caught in the grouting of the stones and along the window ledges. It whipped in a fine spray from spikes on top of a surrounding, iron fence. The brick walks into the building were trodden with snowy footprints, and, at intervals, heavy, snow-moving equipment rumbled down adjoining streets.

Inside, with the exception of a few offices, the building was warm. Too warm. Coughing radiators fought draughts from the poorly fitting, wood-framed windows, and the rubber mats just inside each exterior door glistened from fresh melted snow stamped from innumerable boots. The corridors steamed with the smell of wet wool and leather.

In the dean's outer office, Mrs. Ackerman was at her post. She was a plump, cheerful woman in her mid fifties, of medium height and invariably dressed in a floral print dress. As the dean's secretary, she had been at work since nine o'clock, intermittently typing on her computer for almost two hours. After replacing a folder in a file cabinet, she knocked tentatively on the dean's door and then stood in the open doorway to remind him that a State Department visitor was expected at any moment.

Foreign visitors to the school were usually law-trained, high government officials or emissaries of one sort or another who often were, or had been, engaged in legal education. When the local State Department Visitors Bureau saw these credentials, they invariably thought a visit to a law school would be appropriate.

A few moments later, Mrs. Ackerman again knocked on the door and then entered. Experiencing one of her frowzy intervals, she had met the scheduled visitors and now ushered them into the dean's office. Waving a pencil in her right hand, she announced: "I have the honor of introducing you to the dean of the law school – Dean Massoud Ansari."

As usual, Mrs. Ackerman had forgotten the visitors' names. But as she stood, beaming, the State Department interpreter, an impeccably dressed man of middle age and medium build, stepped forward with his hand outstretched. "Hi, I'm Fred Schmetzkalb," he said. "I'd like to introduce you, Dean, to our visitor, Alhaji Baba Shoppa."

The foreign dignitary also shook the dean's hand. Or, rather, he engulfed it in his own, all the while flashing a broad, ivoried smile. He was a curious, resplendent and incongruous figure. Alhaji Baba Shoppa was from a West African nation. A large – indeed, immense – man with jet-black skin and open, broad and kindly features, he was clad in a long, flowing white robe. Beneath it were a pair of rubber galoshes, and on his head was a wool watch cap.

The dean motioned the two men to the couch to be seated and took an adjoining chair for himself. Before sitting, Mr. Schmetzkalb unbuttoned his jacket to achieve both comfort and an air of informality. Alhaji Baba Shoppa slouched down heavily, his ample posterior vanishing into the couch cushion. He removed his cap and reclined against a pillow, arranging his robe carefully around his legs.

Mrs. Ackerman remained standing in the center of the room.

"Uh, Mrs. Ackerman," the dean said, "thank you."

At this dismissal, she looked reproachful. The dean quickly added: "Perhaps our visitors would like some coffee."

"Oh yes," responded Mrs. Ackerman, "perhaps you would like some coffee." She said this loudly, presumably so that the foreign guest would understand.

The interpreter said something in a strange tongue, and there was a brief response. "Only one coffee," Mr. Schmetzkalb said. "For me."

"How do you take it?" asked Mrs. Ackerman, again a touch too loud.

"Just a little milk, or whatever you have that passes for milk." Mr. Schmetzkalb laughed pleasantly.

Mrs. Ackerman departed, having ascertained that the dean would also take a cup.

Then the three men sat, looking at each other. A nearby curtain wavered slightly, troubled by a draft of wind that whispered through a chink between the window and its frame.

In order to break the ice and end the silence, the dean inquired of Mr. Schmetzkalb, "How does our visitor like to be addressed?"

"Just call him Bobby. He knows that Americans like to use first names, and often the shorter the better. So Bobby will do."

"Okay.... " For a moment, the dean seemed uncertain., but he ploughed forward. "Well, Bobby, how do you like it here in this country?"

Tilting his head to the side and backward, Alhaji Baba Shoppa stared at the dean. Mr. Schmetzkalb, as far as the dean could tell, deftly interpreted his question.

There was a voluble response. It appeared that Alhaji Baba Shoppa indeed liked America and had visited many times. Mr. Schmetzkalb interjected a comment, and the African again subjected his interpreter to a torrent of words. Yes, in fact, Alhaji Baba Shoppa had been to this very city on many occasions. He grinned and spread his giant hands in a deprecatory gesture. Mr. Schmetzkalb also smiled, albeit hesitatingly, and added that Alhaji Baba Shoppa had a romantic interest, and, as you know how American women are, it was necessary to pay frequent attention. It appeared that he had been in the city several days before, had left to attend to business, and had only now just returned with his State Department host.

This conversation was accomplished with an excessive amount of smiling and head bobbing. In dealing with foreign dignitaries, the dean had learned that words through an interpreter convey a message slowly and poorly, so that body language, much the way a dog wags its tail, is the necessary substitute.

Through his interpreter, Allhaji Baba Shoppa asked about the curriculum and admission to the bar. Dean Ansari responded at length, pausing for the appropriate translations. After a while the visitor appeared distracted, and the dean noticed that he kept looking at his watch. Being from a former French colony, his French was excellent. But the conversation was in English, and he appeared impatient with the time it took to interpret remarks in both directions.

Finally, with a smile and an apologetic remark about his ability to converse in English, he asked a question of his own.

It followed several back-and-forth translations about law school administration and the recent, nationwide decline in applications to law schools.

"There are, perhaps, problems with the finance?" Alhaji Baba Shoppa looked at the dean keenly.

"No," the dean answered, attempting an air of imperturbability. "Well, maybe, but nothing to worry about."

Alhaji Baba Shoppa bobbed his massive head. There was an awkward interlude of silence. But again the broad, disarming grin. He cleared his throat, as if prepared to change the subject.

At this moment Mrs. Ackerman reappeared, carrying two cups of coffee. She handed one to the dean and turned to Mr. Schmetzkalb. As she did, the low heel on her shoe caught the edge of a small oriental rug on the floor before the couch where the two visitors were seated. She lurched. A dollop of coffee fell on Alhaji Baba Shoppa's white robe.

"Oh dear. Oh, I'm so very sorry," she cried. The visitor's lips curled inward, and his eyebrows knotted. "I can take care of it."

So saying, she ran from the room, reappearing in a few moments with a wad of wet paper towels in her hand. Before anyone could stop her, she grabbed the robe, much the way she would have grasped an old sheet, and began to rub the offending spot. A soiled, brownish, wet ring spread outward on his robe just below the knee.

This time Alhaji Baba Shoppa looked not so much annoyed as alarmed. His brow knitting with irritation, he grabbed his apparel and wrenched it from Mrs. Ackerman's grasp. "Imbecile," he snorted. She rose from her kneeling position, realizing that she had given offense, and stood for a moment, uncertain what to do. Then, almost dropping the wad of towels, she retreated with flustered apologies from the room.

"Well, Bobby", the dean said, lamely attempting to make amends, "accidents happen. That spot's going to be a bit chilly when you get outdoors." He laughed in an effort to smooth over the situation, and, after a scowl at the empty doorway, Alhaji Baba Shoppa, and then the bewildered interpreter, joined him.

The conversation resumed. Mr. Schmetzkalb reasserted his role as interpreter. Having already discussed issues related to law school administration, the dean asked about life in West Africa. A cordial and lively interchange followed, and for several minutes the dean and his guest traded animated questions and answers interspersed with bursts of laughter. At one point Alhaji Baba Shoppa slapped his thigh in merriment as he recalled an incident as a boy in his home village. And the dean had his own boyhood adventures to relate.

Mr. Schmetzkalb, sitting to one side and busy translating, observed that both men were clearly enjoying each other's company. Eventually, however, he had to interrupt them. "My goodness," he said, feigning surprise, "I think we've overstayed our welcome. We've got to be moving along. This has been most informative."

Saying something in a foreign language to Alhaji Baba Shoppa, he rose to depart, buttoning his jacket.

The dean rose also. "It's certainly been interesting," he said.

Mr. Schmetzkalb translated this remark, and Alhaji Baba Shoppa smiled genially, holding out his large, fleshy hand in farewell. Although he had enjoyed their talk, he had another appointment, evidenced by the number of times he had peeked at his watch. His romantic interest was waiting to join him for lunch as a prelude to a delightful afternoon.

The dean walked the two visitors to the door of his office. "Just let me know, Bobby, if you need more information, and don't let that wet spot get too cold."

There were two desks in the outer office. Mrs. Ackerman, who was seated at the one nearest to the door to the dean's office, rose from her chair and moved around it as the two men appeared. With sincerity and warmth of feeling, she fastened onto Alhaji Baba Shoppa's arm. "I'm so sorry," she said, "about spilling the coffee. I hope you'll forgive me."

Then she withdrew her hand, having forgotten that she had just sharpened several soft-lead pencils and that graphite soot from the lead was on her fingers. This was transferred to his white robe, and both she and the visitor stared at the dark, visible smudge.

With a sharp intake of breath that emerged as a hiss, Alhaji Baba Shoppa quickly drew back his arm and recoiled backward. Muttering "idiot," he put on his watch cap and, clutching his damp robe in one hand, marched out the door to the hallway, followed by Mr. Schmetzkalb.

Mrs. Ackerman stared after them, abashed. The steady thump of galoshes receded down the hall. With a sigh and a shrug, she resumed her seat before her computer.

"That was a little strange," the dean said to her.

"In what way?" She sounded defensive.

"I'm not sure. Why did he ask about our financial situation? Which reminds me. I need to meet as soon as possible with the members of the Financial Aid Committee. If they're in and you can reach them, see if they can meet me in my office."

The clock was ticking. The time was 11:40 am.

Chapter Four

A Revelation and a Warning

"Did you reach the student members of the committee," the dean asked Mrs. Ackerman after the guests had left.

"I couldn't find them," she answered, "I left word with the faculty members, but Richard is in class."

The dean looked at a clock on the wall. "He should be getting out about now. I'll go and intercept him. I need at least some members present for a few minutes. If anyone shows up while I'm gone, tell them I'll be right back."

After ascertaining the correct classroom, the dean walked rapidly to it. Panting from exertion, he paused hesitantly outside to peer through a smoky pane of glass in the door. He could see that the class was ending, and after quietly opening the door, he crept inside and stood in the rear of the room.

The dean wondered why Richard was never called Dick, but that may have been because he was commonly referred to as Mattress Head. At this moment, he had just concluded teaching a class in Criminal Law II, a course for students who wished to study criminal law in greater depth. Some cynics thought it was also for those who wanted an easy grade. Mattress Head, with egalitarian notions firmly implanted from the decade of the sixties, had great difficulty flunking unworthy students. A blank sheet of paper in answer to an examination question – or perhaps one with "Your mother smells bicycle seats" or "Eat It, Prof" scrawled across the middle – might do the trick, but little else. He was the despair of his less charitable, more rigorous colleagues, but someone had to uphold the banner of concern for the disadvantaged – or, as was too often the case, the advantaged who were slothful, indifferent, ungrammatical and bored.

The dean scanned the familiar room and noted that it was too large for the course's modest enrollment. The classrooms at Crabshaw were in consonance with the general decor of the building. That is to say, they were shabby and shopworn in a comfortable sort of way. Located at the rear of the building, this particular room had several rows of tiered desks and seats in a semi-circle around a well with an old table in it. Behind the table in front, and along the side walls, interspersed among elongated, latticed windows, were portraits of bygone men in flowing black robes. Ancestor worship! It was the style of Harvard Law School, with its rows of paintings of former Supreme Court Justices and other illustrious judges lining the walls of its classrooms. At Crabshaw, however, most dignitaries were at the Municipal Court level, and in the rear, unilluminated and unsolicited, hung an oil pointing of a generous graduate who had made it big in the used car business. Someone had decked him out in judicial finery for his portrait, and his hearty, bluff countenance, with just a hint of rapacity in the eyes, gazed down on the congregated students.

After shuffling his papers into a neat pile, Mattress Head started up an aisle after the departing students. An effete man, tall and of slender build, he had a red scarf flung casually about his neck. Above a ragged, unkempt beard, a hawk nose and sunken, sad, gray eyes, a copious mane of dark hair crowded in wild profusion about his head.

He was intercepted by the dean. "I need to speak with you in my office," he said in a low voice. "It's a matter of some urgency."

Puzzled, Mattress Head followed the dean through the open door at the back of the room and up two flights of stairs. Upon entering the dean's outer office, they saw His Jollity, the faculty Chair of the Financial Aid Committee, standing by Mrs. Ackerman's desk. His Jollity had arrived at the school in mid-morning, as was his habit, the clemency or inclemency of the weather never interfering with his relaxed schedule. He was bantering with a student, Prigley Sassoon. They had met each other in the hallway outside the office.

Prigley was a frequent, if not always willing, visitor to the dean's office. He hailed from West Virginia. A stocky young man of medium height, with a bluff, cheerful countenance and guileless manner, he was wearing blue jeans draped too low across his bottom. As a result, his ill-fitting work shirt failed to disguise the elastic top of underpants peeking above his belt. He was also wearing a pair of old loafers and mismatched socks.

Not that Prigley minded – or, to use his vernacular, not that he paid no mind. He did not think he was either well or poorly dressed. If history was any guide, the matter never occurred to him.

His Jollity, who was looking up at his companion, was laughing heartily. He had told the dean once that he thought Prigley was a character, and he enjoyed their conversations. With ink staining his shirt from a pen in his breast pocket, he was as oblivious as Prigley to appearances and unaware that the similarities between them might outweigh the differences.

"Got me an A in Evidence last semester," Prigley was

saying. "How about that? Now I'm going to get me a woman to live with and help me study." He winked.

"Perhaps she could press your pants, too."

"My pants?" With a baffled expression, Prigley studied His Jollity. Then it dawned that he was being teased. "Oh, sure, Prof, but I got something more in mind than laundry." And he laughed – a deep, friendly rumble that started somewhere in his gut and ended somewhere in the back of his throat.

"Don't let me interrupt you," the dean said, interrupting them, but we have business to conduct. Glancing at Prigley, he added: "What brings you here?"

Prigley swallowed his cheerful expression. "I came to apologize for my behavior last week and to talk, maybe, just a little bit more. I'll come back another time."

"Why don't you have Mrs. Ackerman schedule an appointment? Any time later in the week should be fine." The dean then motioned to Mattress Head and His Jollity, and they entered his office. He shut the door quietly but firmly, then waved his visitors to the couch while he drew up a chair on the opposite side of the coffee table.

The men facing him were a picture in contrast. Mattress Head was frowning and ill at ease, but His Jollity settled down with a cheerful grunt, throwing a soft, plump arm up along the back of a pillow. He was a man of instant affability. Short and beefy, his body resembled a squat tree trunk that, if stretched with block and tackle, might rise slightly higher than five foot five inches. Perched on this form was a round head topped by a mop of russet hair and punctuated by a set of twinkling eyes beneath bushy eyebrows. He laughed easily and often.

Looking first of at one, then the other, the dean opened the conversation: "I'm nearly certain there's a problem in our financial aid budget, and because you both are members of the committee, I hoped you might know what's going on. As best I can tell, we seem to be missing about seventy-five thousand dollars a year for the last two or three years. Have you any idea how this has happened? The problem may be worse, once we dig further into it."

Mattress Head and His Jollity exchanged glances. The former spoke: "We meet often to review the awards, and, as you know, being on this committee is a great deal of work. Speaking for myself, I wasn't aware of any problem." He turned to His Jollity. "Were you"?

"No, l thought everything was fine."

Dean Ansari more than anyone was aware that the committee seldom met, and its oversight was perfunctory. No doubt the thief, if there was one, relied on this laxity. Who better than the committee members to detect a discrepancy or, for that matter, arrange for an unauthorized, surreptitious withdrawal? Putting on the horn-rimmed glasses that dangled precariously from a slender, black wisp of braided string about his neck, he studied each man. The possibility seemed highly unlikely – indeed, remote. Still, he had hoped for an inadvertent clue or an explanation; none was forthcoming.

"Thomas Headly might have given me the answer," the dean continued, "but I'm sure you've both heard about the unfortunate accident."

"If it was an accident," His Jollity said.

The dean swung around to peer at him. Mattress Head gazed at His Jollity intently, his sunken eyes accentuated by his prominent nose.

"What do you mean?" Mattress Head ventured before the

dean could speak. "The papers reported that he fell through his apartment window after a party."

"Yes, they did," His Jollity responded. "But yesterday I spoke with Kevin Pannelli in my office. You know him; he's a student member of this committee, and partly because of that, we've become pretty well acquainted. He was kind of agitated and asked if I could set up a meeting with you, Dean, and the entire committee. Thomas had told him some things and given him some papers we would want to see. He said that Thomas wasn't at that party for very long and that he didn't like to drink. Also, that he usually kept his living room window only partially open because his apartment was so hot."

There was a moment of silence. "How far open?"

"I don't know."

"Are you saying he might not have fallen through it? Did the police check?"

"I don't know that either. Let's hear what Kevin has to say."

"My God," the dean whispered. Mattress Head continued to stare at His Jollity, then musingly wiped his hand in a tugging motion across his bearded chin.

"For the time being, we shouldn't talk about this with anyone," the dean said softly. "We can discuss it with the police as soon as we've had a meeting, and we'd better have one as soon as possible. Did Thomas speak with Ruth?"

"Ruth? Ruth who?"

"You know, Ruth Dinsmore, the other student member of the committee."

"Oh, right," His Jollity said. "I don't know that either."

"I'll ask Mrs. Ackerman to contact every member of the committee and order some sandwiches. We can meet here for lunch – let's say around 12:30. Any problem with that?"

Both men shook their heads from side to side. After a pause, Mattress Head rose to depart, but His Jollity remained seated. "I'd like to talk with you about something personal," he said to the dean. "This is probably about as good a time as any, unless you're too busy."

"I don't have any other appointments this morning." Mattress Head had grasped the door handle and was about to turn it. "Please shut the door behind you, Richard, so we can speak without interruption. I'll see you in a half hour or so… even if we can't find Kevin and Ruth."

The dean was seated on a cushioned, wooden chair, his elbows on the protruding arms and the tips of his fingers touching in a spindly tent, his forefingers pressed together on his chin just below his lower lip. Dropping his hands and stretching out his legs, he looked at His Jollity. "Thanks very much for looking around your office to see if anything was stolen. I gather you haven't discovered anything."

"No, nothing is missing, as far as I can tell. You said someone was in my office? I wonder why."

"So do I. He may have been looking for something to steal and was interrupted. But I'm not sure how he got in. You do keep it locked when you leave, don't you?"

"Absolutely." Hesitantly, His Jollity added, "Under the circumstances, I'd like to request that Maintenance put in a new lock as soon as possible."

"There's a form to fill out. I'll have Mrs. Ackerman see to it. Anyway, for the time being, keep it to yourself. We have enough trouble attracting students without raising concerns about safety."

His Jollity said, "I'm afraid that cat's out of the bag. There are rumors floating around already. But nobody seems to know what really happened."

"Good. Let's keep it that way." The dean's comment was followed by an interval of silence. Staring down at the carpet, he cleared his throat. "So – what's on your mind?"

His Jollity's budding dewlap quivered, and he puckered his lips attentively. To match his stocky frame, he should have had a gravely, deep voice; instead, nature had conferred upon him the incongruous, adolescent vocal chords of a pubescent boy. "When you became dean," he said, the words juxtaposed in a contralto singsong, "I gave you some advice. Do you remember?"

"I'm not sure… I think so."

"I told you that in this job you were inevitably bound to use up your political capital, which most of the time means deciding for one person against another or one group against another. People on the downside of those decisions get resentful. And, you know, you're dealing with people who never go away and never forget. With a mostly tenured faculty, they're always around to get back at you, and you've got to keep living with them. Look," he continued, "the folks in our part of the building know just as well as you that this place has troubles, and I'm beginning to sense that many faculty members wonder whether you have the will and resolution to surmount them. Losing money in financial aid sure isn't going to help. I think there's a good deal of unrest, but I hesitated to say anything, because, frankly, I'm not sure what you can do about it… You don't have many options. Maybe, though, you could come down harder on some of us who don't work as hard as we ought."

His Jollity had Windy Dave in mind. The dean had learned that when faculty members made this kind of comment, they always had Windy Dave in mind. Windy Dave was an elderly professor with a ruddy complexion and a luxuriant mane of wavy, white hair. When he spoke, the sonorous sound was akin to stirring molasses: slow, deliberate and infinitely tedious.

"It's easier," the dean answered, "to recommend coming down hard than to do it. For one thing, I'm not sure it works. If morale is bad, it will only make it worse." His stomach clenched. *When this place goes down the tubes, and I'm pulled down the whirlpool with it, what will happen to me?*

"It can work, I think, if done properly," His Jollity said.

"What? Oh, yes… of course, of course." Confused, having lost the thread of the conversation, the dean groped for a way back in. "You and Prigley Sassoon seem…" He never concluded the sentence. A sharp knock on the door was followed, immediately thereafter, by the unannounced entrance of Bathroom Bob. He looked more than usually agitated, and he barged in, brushing his straight, blond hair back from a thin face slightly disfigured by pockmarks left from teen-age acne. A wispy mustache straggled beneath a pinched nose that angled slightly to one side.

Bathroom Bob had originally acquired his nickname from his habit of always using an out-of-the-way lavatory in the basement. For that reason, his name at first had been Basement Bathroom Bob, or B Cubed, but from long usage students had shortened it to Bathroom Bob, or B Squared.

He was the third faculty member on the Financial Aid Committee.

"Ah, you've come," the dean said cheerfully. "I'm glad you got the note. We'll have another meeting… "

He got no farther. Bathroom Bob did not pause to observe social amenities or apologize for his interruption. Instead, he burst out, "I am sick and tired… I tell you, I am sick and tired… of the unsanitary conditions in the men's room."

His voice was strident. When speaking, particularly if agitated, he had a tendency to stop abruptly in mid-sentence, often more than once, so that his words, though uttered quickly, were delivered with individual emphasis in staccato cadence, as if each syllable and thought was uniquely important.

"This place is a pig pen anyway," he went on. "The faculty don't have a separate john... we're all mixed in there like cattle... and anyone can walk in off the street."

He did not add, "and what are you going to do about it?" although that was the clear import of the tirade. Astonished, the dean's mouth was agape. It was a moment, as in the old comic strips, when the hero, caught unawares, says "What the...?" just before being bopped on the head. Bathroom Bob seemed to be insisting that the dean add the duties of watchman and public health inspector to his decanal chores.

His Jollity was immobile, cheeks at rest, blinking impassively at the intruder. After a moment, he said: "For Christ's sake, what's the matter? Take it easy. Hey, Bob, take it easy."

Exhaling through tightly pursed lips, Bathroom Bob seemed to see him for the first time. Because his neck hung forward as if he were ducking under a low-hanging branch, he appeared to be looking up at His Jollity. "I've had it... and a lot you care... or most of the people in this ridiculous excuse for a law school." He spat his words, eyes staring intently from his cocked head. "Anybody uses that bathroom... they don't wash their hands... at least we have toilet seat covers in the booths... there ought to be a dispenser with towelettes for holding the urinal handles when you flush... I have to use a paper towel which I get over by the sinks... today I used one... and a student laughed... you all think it's funny... and I'm sick and tired of it."

Use a paper towel? Hesitating, the dean queried: "You don't think there are germs on the handles, do you? You're not going to catch anything, Bob."

The remark was kerosene thrown on a wood fire. "Catch anything?" Bathroom Bob screeched. "You're damn right I'll catch something... where have you been? People touch themselves in there... haven't you ever heard of AIDS, or herpes, or... or...?"

"Yes, but you aren't going to catch them by flushing the urinal. Come on, Bob. This conversation reminds me of the definition of a religious man: that's someone who washes his hands *before* going to the bathroom."

The attempt at humor failed. Bathroom Bob glared at him.

"I knew I wouldn't get anywhere," he muttered.

But His Jollity had recovered from the wild interruption, and a look of comprehension, even sympathetic understanding, illuminated his face. In a genial, mollifying tone, he said, "You know, Bob, I first encountered this problem when I was in law practice. The building our firm was in had a bathroom like the ones here. Anyone could use it. And just about anyone did. I figured out a way to flush the urinals without touching the handles with my hands."

Surely, dear God, the dean thought, even at Crabshaw, there can't be two people like this.

His Jollity continued. "You see, what you do is, first, you only use a urinal next to a booth. Then, after you've finished, you grab the top of the side of the booth and hoist yourself up. You can flush the urinal by extending your leg and depressing the handle with your foot. Like this."

So saying, he grasped the top side of an imaginary booth and, pirouetting in a quarter circle, with his leg kicked out beside him, delicately inclined his foot toward an imaginary handle. Finished, he dropped his leg, turned a nearby, imaginary spigot and began laving his hands in an imaginary basin.

Bathroom Bob viewed him intently. Animosity and frustration had vanished from his features, replaced by a look of appreciative concentration.

"I'm not sure," he said. "Will the side of the booth hold me?"

"Sure," answered His Jollity, "I do it all the time."

"What if someone in there sees your fingertips and thinks you're about to climb in over the side?"

"Ask him to pay no attention. Tell him it will only take a few seconds. The person sitting in there won't mind."

"What if he does? What if he objects?"

"Just tell him you're a professor. There won't…"

"Like this, you say?" interrupted Bathroom Bob. Standing at one side of the table, he reached his arms up, lifted one leg and spun around. His outstretched leg nearly collided with the dean's balding head..

"Oh, sorry Dean… I was just trying to see how you do it."

"No problem." Having jerked his head backward, the dean readjusted it to a normal position. "Listen, why don't you two fellows… Ow! Damn it!" The word damn was accentuated. Bathroom Bob had lowered his leg abruptly, stepping in the process on one of the dean's neatly polished shoes.

"God damn it!" Dean Ansari rose, hopped in a circle, banged into the coffee table, then sat heavily back down.

Mrs. Ackerman appeared at the door, alarm on her face. "Is everything all right?"

"Yes, yes," the dean puffed. "Bob just stepped on one of my feet. As I was saying, or trying to say – dammit, that hurts – why don't you two go to the bathroom for a lesson."

"Are you okay?" asked His Jollity.

"Yes. No problem. Really. Just caught one of my corns. Got them, you know."

His Jollity did not know. "Come on, let's go to the men's room," he said to Bathroom Bob. "We'll use the one in the basement. I'll show you how it's done." He paused. "We should have just enough time to practice and be back here at 12:30."

The two men rose, chatting amiably, to commence Bob's inaugural lesson on the use of feet to achieve proper hygiene. As they were leaving, His Jollity turned to the dean: "You're sure you're all right?"

"Yes, I'm fine," the dean said, slowly shaking his head. "Don't take too long." The cramp in his stomach, now worse, returned.

It was a few minutes after twelve noon.

Chapter Five

An Unexpected Discovery

Without the courtesy of a warning knock, His Jollity and Bathroom Bob burst unasked through the door to the dean's inner office not five minutes after their departure. They had brushed past Mrs. Ackerman without glance or comment. Through the door, now ajar, the dean could see that she had risen and was staring at them around the corner, a look of concern on her face.

The dean was sitting behind his desk talking on the telephone with a lady friend, but Bathroom Bob's putty-colored face and obvious agitation were prompting enough to terminate the conversation. "I seem to have some kind of emergency here," he said into the receiver. "I'll get back to you as soon as I can." He placed the telephone in its cradle. "What's the matter? Why are you back so soon?"

Bathroom Bob opened his mouth to speak, his eyes bulging from a head twisted sharply to the side, but no words emerged. His Jollity, who was standing directly behind his compatriot, his cheeks appearing not fleshy but sunken, spoke after clearing his throat. His boyish intonation was deeper, huskier. "We... went to the bathroom in the basement because... because we thought, you know, that there might be more privacy there... and... and when we walked in... when we walked in there was Kevin lying on the floor... and there was blood all over the place... and we think... I mean, I think, but I'm sure Bob agrees… we think that he's dead… and we ran back here."

"Kevin? Kevin who? Not Kevin Pannelli."

"Yes, Kevin Pannelli." His Jollity was panting from his recent exertion, and his voice rose as he spoke.

"We'd better get down there. Maybe he's still alive."

He rose hastily, almost tipping over his chair. ""Mrs. Ackerman! Mrs. Ackerman!" he called sharply. Trying to act as if she had not been eavesdropping, she ducked back, then reappeared at the door, aware from his urgent shout and the little she had overheard that some catastrophe had occurred. "You'd better call an ambulance… no, wait… no, do it right now." He was thinking rapidly, thoughts cascading on top of each other in a welter of confusion. "It may not be necessary… but go ahead… I'll be right back."

Dean Ansari ran into the corridor outside his office and headed for the stairwell at the opposite end.. Two steps at a time, he raced down the stairs until he came at last to a passageway in the basement.

It was poorly illuminated – a fact he barely noticed. He flicked on lights as His Jollity, panting even harder, and Bathroom Bob emerged from the stairwell behind him. On either side of the corridor for half its length were student lockers, but classes were in session, and no students were there removing books or putting on coats and hats before leaving the building. Near the end a smaller passageway entered from a furnace room, and just inside this passageway to the right was the janitor's office. The door was closed. To the left was the men's room that had been the genesis of Bathroom Bob's name. Beyond this bathroom and the janitor's office was a large storage area occupied by used, empty file cabinets and broken-down chairs and desks. Overhead was a lattice of pipes, large and small in diameter, wrapped in insulation and raddled across the ceiling. The space was dingy, and the hiss and clank of the furnace just beyond the storage space muffled the sound of their running footsteps on the linoleum floor.

The dean saw a bright line of illumination angling from beneath the bathroom door. He shoved it open. Later, he remembered the vivid color red against the white sinks and the small, white, hexagonal tiles on the floor. It was like vermilion splashed on a blank canvas. Blood was spattered against a wall that was smeared by a slippery handprint dragged downward to the floor. Underneath, sprawled in an ungainly posture, lay a young man. He was lying crumpled on his back a few feet from the half-opened door of an unoccupied toilet stall, and his trousers and underpants had been pulled down to his knees. His pale penis flopped lazily to one side in the dark, curly hair that surrounded it, and for a moment the dean felt compelled to cover him.

Instead, he dropped to one knee and listened to detect breath. There was none. He reached for the young man's wrist to feel for pulse, and at that moment, glancing at the face, he confirmed that it was Kevin Pannelli, one of his students. The eyes stared upward, unblinking. The entire left side of his face and head was covered with blood. It was oozing from a hideous gash above his left ear, matting his hair and spreading in a widening pool on the tiled floor.

The dean stood, stepped back and, with a grimace, glanced at his hands, trousers and polished shoes to check whether, inadvertently, he had touched or stepped in any of the blood. Then he looked at his watch; it was 12:15, just after the noon hour. For the first time, he was aware of the room's brightness and a faint buzzing from the overhead, fluorescent lights. He glanced at the empty stall, then with a start noticed a pair of women's shoes behind the closed door of the one next to it.

"Whoever you are," he said in a low, tremulous voice, "come out of there."

There was no sound.

"I said, come out."

No response.

Cautiously, the dean turned the handle. The door swung slowly outward. The shoes were empty. Propped against the back of the toilet tank was a Raggedy Andy doll. With its bright, unblinking eyes and fixed grin, it was staring at the corpse on the floor in front of the adjacent stall as though amused at the drollery of the scene.

Stumbling backward, the dean shouted at the doorway where His Jollity was standing. "I need some help here."

"Is he dead?"

"I'm not... yes, I think so. You... you stay here outside the door, and don't let anyone in. And don't touch anything. Tell Bob to stay with you. I'm going back upstairs and make sure an ambulance is on the way, although I don't think we need one. And the police... I'm going to call the police."

Bathroom Bob had remained outside the door. He was leaning, wordless, against a wall, his head crooked to one side. Having removed his glasses, he was wiping the side of his forehead with the palm of his hand when His Jollity grasped him by the elbow. Together, they retreated to the end of the small passageway where it entered the main corridor, a place with greater visibility in case the assailant – or assailants – was still lurking nearby.

The dean walked past them and hurried back along the

central corridor. A couple of students, having recently arrived, were busily removing books from their lockers and waved a cheery hello. As he approached the first landing, he noticed that a heavy, metal door to an adjacent parking lot was slightly ajar. The wind had sprayed snow through the narrow gap in an elongated triangle across the floor. Heaving on the crash bar, he closed the door and only then recalled that he had heard a car, its tires spinning on the snow, trying to exit the parking lot as he had been running downstairs.

To Mrs. Ackerman, back in his office, the dean issued the urgent command that the police be summoned at once. He did not, for the moment, tell her the reason. He also asked her to call the local hospital and make sure an ambulance had been dispatched. Baffled and alarmed, she complied. "When they arrive," he said, "tell them to come in. I'll be waiting in my office."

And it was there that he retired, the perplexities and absurdities of the morning forgotten. Agitated, moisture in his palms, he stood by his high window, peering through the wavering lace of descending snow for a sign of flashing lights on the road leading to the school.

Kevin Pannelli, he thought, bowing his head against the coolness of the windowpane. Who could have done such a dreadful thing? And how? And why Kevin Pannelli?

Chapter Six

Lieutenant McCallister

Two black and white cruisers pulled up in front of the law school, and three blue-uniformed men got out and walked down the rutted path through falling snow to the front entrance of the school. Once inside, a flustered Mrs. Ackerman greeted them.

"Officers. Thank goodness you're here. Something terrible has apparently happened. I don't know what, but it's something really terrible. This way, please, this way."

The leader of the group, a sergeant, smiled. "It's okay, ma'am. Calm down. Who's the head person here?"

At that moment Dean Ansari emerged from his office, and Mrs. Ackerman pointed to him. This time there was no flourish, no grand introduction. The three men, grim-faced, waited as he approached and introduced himself. He explained what he had seen. The sergeant, after hearing his description, sent one of the men back to his car to fetch tape and then punched a speed number on his cell phone.

"We've got a problem here," he said. "It may be an accident, but a witness thinks it's a homicide. Is McCallister there?" There was a long pause. "Yeah, he thinks he's dead. They've called an ambulance.... Okay, come to the basement. I'll ask someone at the front door to show you the way."

Within minutes, a third cruiser arrived, lights flashing, and this time two men in civilian clothes emerged. After inquiring at the entrance, they descended immediately to the basement corridor. There the dean, the sergeant and one of the patrolmen were waiting. The other patrolman, who had gone to his car, was already sealing off the area with yellow tape. His Jollity and Bathroom Bob were standing to one side.

"Are you the boss?" one of the men in civilian clothes said, addressing his question to the dean.

"Yes, I'm Dean Ansari."

"I'm Lieutenant Antwan McCallister," the man said, "and this is my partner, Joe Walsh. Show me the body… and don't touch anything."

Lieutenant McCallister was a tall, slender African American with a pencil-thin mustache and a receding hairline. Dressed in a charcoal gray suit, he had already removed his overcoat and draped it over his right arm. His companion was a middle aged white man of medium height with an unkempt, full beard and a large paunch. He had on a black, thick, wool overcoat and a fedora, which he removed, revealing a shock of iron gray hair.

The dean escorted the two detectives into the men's room. When he saw the body, Lieutenant Walsh whistled. "Yup," he said, "it doesn't look good."

Lieutenant McCallister dropped to one knee and examined the wound, slowly nodding his head. "Blunt force trauma," he muttered, "and really bad. It happened recently. Still warm." He stood, turned around, and for the first time saw the woman's shoes and the grinning, Raggedy Andy doll. His companion was already staring at the scene, open-mouthed.

"What the hell is this?" Lieutenant McCallister said. He turned to the dean. "Was this here when you found the body?" He received a nod of affirmation in reply.

Lieutenant Walsh spoke. "It sure doesn't look like an accident. More like some kind of ritual murder, if you ask me."

Lieutenant McCallister clamped his lips and shrugged. "Could be," he muttered. "Could be. Let's get some photographs," he barked at one of the officers. "We're going to have to examine the body and comb this area thoroughly… and impound evidence like that fucking doll… and those shoes."

For the first time he seemed to notice His Jollity and Bathroom Bob. "Who're these guys?" he inquired of the dean.

"They're professors here at the law school. They were the first ones to find the body… as far as we know. Not me. They've been here watching to make sure no one entered the corridor." The dean indicated the small hallway leading to the men's room, storage area and furnace room.

"Good. You see anyone?"

"No. No, sir," Bathroom Bob spoke. "No one came in or out."

"After we get this area secured," Lieutenant McCallister said, "I'm going to want to talk to you. And to you, too, Dean. Please make yourselves available." He walked outside the men's room. "Okay, that's it. Let's get to work."

The dean turned to go. A small crowd of students, speaking in hushed whispers, had gathered near the yellow tape, and more were arriving. He pushed his way through them and returned to his office.

* * * * *

Lieutenant McCallister had settled into an end cushion on the dean's couch. He had hung his overcoat on the clothes tree by the door, and his gray suit and subdued, crimson tie complemented the dean's conservative attire. Joe Walsh was still downstairs supervising a thorough search of the crime scene, including the furnace room, storage area and, when it could be opened, the janitor's office. So far, he reported that he and his men had not found any clues.

"You say his name was Kevin Pannelli?"

"Yes," the dean responded. "He was one of our third year students."

"Did you know him well?"

"No. He was a good student, very friendly, not much more."

"Any known enemies, bad habits?"

"You mean like drugs? As I said, I didn't know him well, but I'd be surprised... And enemies? He was a nice kid. I doubt it."

"Hmmm. How about his friends? Do you know of anyone we could talk to who might give us useful information, personal or otherwise?"

The dean shook his head. "I'm not much help, I guess... Oh, wait, there was one student who knew him, probably a friend. But he fell..." The dean paused. "Well, we think he fell from his living room window and died a few days ago. Actually, a couple of days ago."

"Really?" Lieutenant McCallister blinked, shifted position and withdrew a notebook and pen from his pocket. "Would you give me his name?"

"Sure. It was Thomas Headly. I don't know much about him either, except that he was a good student like Kevin and worked in the university Accounting Office."

"Who'd he work for?"

"It was one of our vice presidents, Allison Fetherheft. She's over on the main campus."

Lieutenant McCallister wrote down the name and a telephone number that the dean supplied.

"Do you know why Kevin was in the basement?"

"No idea. Probably to get books or clothes from his locker. Most of our student lockers are in the hallway leading to the men's room."

"Okay." Lieutenant McCallister fiddled with his pen as he looked at the dean. "Would you mind telling me how you were informed about this crime – I think for the time being we're going to treat it as a homicide – and exactly what you did in response?"

The dean related what had happened, how he had run downstairs, found the body, saw the grinning doll and returned to his office to wait for the police.

"What do you make of that doll?" Lieutenant McCallister queried. "Ever see it before?"

"Never. Or the shoes. I've no idea what that's all about."

After prolonged silence while Lieutenant McCallister scribbled notes in his notebook, the lieutenant asked, "Anything else?"

The dean sat still for a couple of minutes, thinking. His head was bowed, and he tapped his fingers on the sides of his chair. Then he looked up. "Thomas Headly may have given Kevin some papers, but they weren't with the body."

"What kind of papers?"

"I don't know."

"We'll look for them."

"Another thing. I think the door to the outside – the one with the crash bar on the landing – was closed when I went downstairs. Or it may have been open, I'm not sure. Anyway, it was open when I came back. And I heard a car spinning its wheels as it was trying to leave the parking area."

"Did you see it?"

"No. It was probably just a student leaving after class. But I did notice the sound."

"Not much to go on there, I'm afraid." Lieutenant McCallister returned his pen and notebook to a pocket, then scratched his chin. "Anything else?"

"Well, yes. Someone broke into one of our faculty offices a couple of nights ago and scared the wits out of a young, female member of our staff who happened to be there."

"Did he take anything or attack her, I mean, molest her in some way?"

"No, they just stared at each other and then he walked – or I guess ran – to an interior stairwell." The dean paused. "She said that, as he was walking by her, he told her it was her lucky night, I guess because he heard me running down the stairs."

Lieutenant McCallister scratched his chin again. He had retrieved his notebook and was busily writing in it. "That's three incidents – a death off campus, maybe accidental, a homicide in your basement and, I suppose, a burglary. That's an impressive list." He cocked his head and looked squarely at the dean. "Do you see any connection? My hunch is that at least a couple of them are connected in some way, although I'll be damned if I see how."

"I hate to add another to the list," the dean said, "but I guess I ought to. I've discovered that some of our financial aid funds are missing. So far I haven't a clue how it happened or who might have done it."

Lieutenant McCallister emitted a low whistle. "That's quite a laundry list. It was impressive to begin with, and now, I guess, you've added embezzlement. To put it mildly, this is getting interesting... I almost hate to ask, but anything else you think we ought to know?"

The dean, who had been leaning forward, smiled faintly. "No, I think that's it. It damn well better be. If this news gets out, our applications for admission are going to dry up completely, and it's bad enough right now."

Lieutenant McCallister surveyed the dean sympathetically. "I'm sorry, Dean. We'll handle any publicity with as much sensitivity as we can." He paused while a gust of wind rattled a window. "Right now I can't think of further questions, so that's it. Thanks very much for your time... for your help. I'm pretty sure I'll want to see you again."

"No problem."

"Oh, one more thing. I noticed the janitor's office is almost directly across the hall from the men's room. It was locked. We're going to need to get in there. Do you know anything about the janitor or where he was at the time the death occurred."

"I'm not much help there. He was hired by the university personnel office – well, we call it Human Resources now – and I really don't know him. I do know, though, that he's usually upstairs working in the morning. For what it's worth, his name is Charles Traynor."

Lieutenant McCallister had been about to put away his notebook and pen. Instead, he stopped and wrote down the name. "Okay, thanks for that. Please send someone to unlock that office." He rose and walked to the door. "Of course," he said, "we'll need to talk with members of your faculty – particularly the ones I met downstairs – but also anyone else who was here this morning. In fact, maybe all of them. Would you mind letting them know that I or Joe will be getting in touch with them?"

The dean had also risen. "I'll see to it," he said. "We'll be as cooperative as we can, and I sure hope we get to the bottom of this mess very soon."

Late Winter into Early Spring: More Trouble from Every Quarter

Chapter Seven

The Plotters

They were seated in Duxbury's office, conferring in hushed tones.

Duxbury had originally been called Baked Bean due to his origin in New England near Boston. But ultimately the town of his birth, alluded to frequently in classroom hypothetical problems, became ascendant. A tall, willowy man with a thatch of receding gray-brown hair and a pointed goatee, somewhat in the style of Leon Trotsky, Duxbury wore square, gold spectacles atop a long, protruding nose. His vices were greed and manipulation, and he imagined himself a conspiratorial, Machiavellian character. In this self-appraisal he was, as in many things, correct.

Boomer was sitting on a large, comfortable chair near Duxbury's desk. Books and papers had been removed from the chair and placed on the floor where they blended with other, similar piles of reading material scattered in layered stacks around the room. Boomer was built like a thick post with oversized hands, feet, ears and jowls. He possessed a glistening head devoid of hair, except for a dark fringe, and an unusually large, mushroom nose spider-webbed with broken capillaries. His nickname derived from his propensity, whenever he was told anything in confidence, to immediately and cheerfully advertise the news, often with bumbling embellishment.

Seated opposite Boomer on a small couch were two other

faculty members, Junker and The Duchess. The former, his nickname conferred by virtue of his close-cropped, bristly hair, should have been a Teutonic Knight, perhaps the Master of a castle in East Prussia. About sixty years of age, of medium height and build, ramrod erect, impeccably attired in a three-piece suit and with piercing blue eyes, Junker was a man who had, somehow, bungled into the wrong century and the wrong occupation. He did not brook vacuous chatter, and a twitching, flaring mustache signaled the end of his tolerance. In most conversations this event occurred quickly.

His companion was mismatched with Junker in nearly every respect. The Duchess had soft, rounded features that perfectly mirrored the contours of her body. A middle-aged, plump woman with graying hair pulled into a bun, she worried openly and often about the students, the school, the profession, her colleagues and herself. Unlike Junker, she was not given to complaints, only anxiety. This trait aside, she was sensible and hard working, and her fellow teachers enjoyed her friendly, albeit sometimes fretful, outlook on life.

"That little figure is a riot," The Duchess exclaimed. "You know, if you look at it a certain way, it almost looks like the dean, and you've even captured the thinning hair." She was referring to a clay figurine near a telephone at the rear of Duxbury's desk that he had molded recently in an art class and had forgotten to replace on his bookshelf. It was of a tall, slightly stooped man, and the attire on the sculpted figure had been clumsily fashioned into a replica of a herringbone jacket, with patches at the elbows.

"Yeah, I suppose it does look like the dean." Junker's piercing eyes surveyed the little figure. "Maybe we should turn its face to the wall."

Duxbury added quickly, "Or up against the wall?"

"No, in a wastepaper basket will do. There's got to be one around here somewhere, although God knows how we'd find it."

There was laughter. It was Boomer who had spoken.

Duxbury, who was seated behind his desk, stretched out his arm, grasped the figurine in his bony hand, and marched it past scattered law books to the edge of his desk. His wastepaper basket was directly underneath. With elaborate slowness, holding fast to the statue, he arced it in a high dive, making the figure disappear beneath the mound of crumpled papers in the overflowing basket.

The Duchess clapped her hands amidst smiles on the surrounding faces. "If I were a judge, I'd give that about a four or five."

Retrieving the figurine, Duxbury sighed. "Well, I guess it wasn't an Olympic performance. But it looked bloody good to me." Then he marched it back to its previous location and, to muted laughter, lay it down on its back.

"Nothing that man does is an Olympic performance," growled Junker. His tone was sour. The laughter died. "The school is in trouble, and now we find a dead body in one of our bathrooms – unfortunately, a good student. We can't afford to lose our good ones with all the dullards to worry about."

"Be fair," interposed Duxbury with a sly smile. "There are some good students."

This comment brought a frosty smile to Junker's face. He started to speak but was interrupted.

"Hi everybody!" The group looked to the doorway, now occupied by Aaron, who had been walking by on his way to his office. Aaron's seldom-used nickname was BN. He looked out at the world through spectacles that resembled the bottoms of soft drink bottles. These glasses rested on a prominent nose that protruded from a thin, pale face under a thatch of dark hair. An easy smile and a clubby tweed jacket on a frail frame barely saved him from social oblivion.

"What's up?"

"Oh, nothing." Two or three voices responded nearly as one.

"Mind if I come in, or..." Aaron hesitated, seeing that no chairs were available, "or stand by the door?"

"Not at all, my dear fellow, not at all," Duxbury answered. "We were just talking about the murder in the basement and the dean." Pausing, he added, "You know, something's got to be done." His geniality vanished as he searched the faces in the room.

"The school has serious problems, and they aren't being solved. We're perceived as a third-rate institution in a third-rate city, and our applications have started to show it. Our alumni are embarrassed to say they went here. They're at the bottom of the pecking order when it comes to getting jobs. And this murder has just made everything much worse."

"Are our applications down very much from last year?" The Duchess stared plaintively in the direction of Boomer, who was Chair of the Admissions Committee. "I'm so worried we're not holding our own. I heard that applications to law schools in the west are holding steady. And now this dreadful murder right in our own basement... right near the student lockers. Did you see all that yellow tape? It was there for days. And we're all being questioned by the police. I wouldn't be surprised if no one wanted to come here."

"And no one's been caught," Junker snorted contemptuously.

"Maybe the dean did it," Boomer joked. "As for our applications," he said, looking at the The Duchess, "yes, they're down a lot. Which means lower enrollment, less tuition revenue, and a very bad impact on our budget. It may mean the jobs of some of us. And you're wrong about schools in the west. The last I heard, applications are down all over but even more here because of our reputation." He shook his massive head.

Staring fixedly at him, Junker looked as if he had just seen an ungainly, black beetle crawl across the wall. He adjusted his small, round, iron glasses. Had he lived in a different era in his beloved Fatherland, he would have vastly preferred exiling all weaker students to Lithuania or, preferably, to one of the former German colonies in Africa.

"So," he said. Ach so, would have been more in character. He seemed, mustache bristling, every inch a stiff Prussian officer or perhaps schoolmaster. However, a monocle and high-starched collar were missing, as was a spiked helmet. "What we have is a deteriorating situation under the command of a tail-wagging, bungling incompetent." That he did not say schweinhund was only an accident of place, time and immigrant grandparents. Junker surveyed the disposition of the school's forces bleakly and concluded, in a few pithy comments, that either a putsch or a general retreat was in order.

"I couldn't agree more." Aaron had been waiting for an opportunity to participate. "It's time we got tough," he said in a nasally, high-pitched voice, punching his right fist into the palm of his other hand. Everyone glanced in his direction, waiting for him to say more. But there was no more.

The silence, prolonged for a moment, was filled by Duxbury. "So, what do we do? How can we remedy this situation?"

"I think we've got to get rid of the dean," replied Boomer. Junker nodded his head. In a moment, Aaron nodded his head, too.

The Duchess, frowning unhappily, gently squeezed the knuckles on her hands. "We have to consider the impact on the school. I mean, this isn't something you do lightly. The students have to be considered. Lots of them like him. And the alumni. And, of course, the staff and the university administration. There could be big trouble, and we don't want to get caught up in it. Let's think this through carefully."

"If I'm not mistaken... and I doubt very much that I am," said Junker, "the president really likes the way he's doing things. They certainly get along with each other. Maybe too much. We need an independent voice as dean, not someone who's always agreeing with Zo when he tears down the faculty."

The president's name was Druzolovic Zo. Someone, once, had joked that his ancestors emigrated from Transylvania, and the joke took root as an enduring myth. Zo himself had alluded once to a great grandfather expelled from Hungary for revolutionary activity against the Emperor Franz Joseph, but he never revisited the subject. The name remained of uncertain origin, and the man was as complex and enigmatic as his name. A veteran of the war in Korea and the retreat from the Yalu River, he survived with the loss of his left leg just below the knee. Yet his ebullience never wavered, and he stumped through his days, beret pulled jauntily to one side over jet-black hair, with good cheer but a noticeable limp on a prosthetic lower limb and foot.

"Yeah, let's face it," said Boomer. "He does get out a lot to talk with people. He told the Board of Trustees last month that we're raising four times as much money every year as we did only a half dozen years ago."

"It must come from all those visitors he has in his office," volunteered Aaron. "Did you see that guy with the long white robe and the funny galoshes who was here about a month ago. An African, from the look of it. He kept brushing his arm as he was leaving the building – I was looking out my window at the snow – and then he sat for the longest time in a car after another man said goodbye and left. He looked awfully unhappy."

"That's probably because the dean just let him pick up the check," laughed Boomer, and the others joined in.

"Give him his due; give him his due," murmured Duxbury, smiling mirthlessly. "Deans are paid to lie. We may be raising four times as much money as before, but we all know that four times zero is still zero, and anyone giving money to the school is on a fool's errand." He doodled on a piece of paper on the desk in front of him while the group fell silent. There was no point, he realized, in talking about academic standards; they had been tightened markedly. There was also no point in discussing the budget that had apparently been kept in balance despite the recent decline in applications and enrollment.

Aaron fidgeted by the door. The Duchess gazed anxiously out the window, while Boomer picked up an elastic band and laced it through his thick fingers, concentrating on the varying patterns as if nothing could be more important. Junker, sitting erect and somber, stared straight ahead.

Duxbury put down his pencil and stopped doodling. "I have an idea," he said, as if the thought had just occurred to him.

Junker looked at Duxbury suspiciously. "What kind of idea?"

Duxbury coughed nervously into his hand. "This murder

is going to really hurt us, and we need someone to help us weather the storm. We need to replace the dean. While I'm very reluctant, I propose myself as the person for the job. On an interim basis, of course, although I wouldn't preclude answering a draft movement by the faculty, should that be forthcoming, to assume the burden permanently."

Once again, there was silence. The small room was palpably quiet. Finally, The Duchess spoke: "Perhaps we could call a meeting of the faculty. We need to talk it over. But I don't want to hurt anybody's feelings. That would be terrible. And we don't want to irritate President Zo."

"Don't worry about Zo," Duxbury said. "I've spoken with him privately."

"You have? What about?" Junker asked eagerly.

"About the dean. Zo's not as big a supporter of him as we used to think. He knows the school is in real trouble. I said maybe we should have a meeting to talk it over, and he agreed. I got the sense that he wouldn't object if we started looking for a new dean."

Again, for a few moments, no one spoke. Duxbury surveyed them benignly. "We don't have to hurt anyone," he continued thoughtfully – and disingenuously. "We're all expressing honest opinions, and there's nothing wrong with being frank and candid. We just need to get our message across to make sure everyone understands."

Boomer glanced around the room. "All right, then," he said, a tinge of excitement in his voice. "We'll call a meeting of the faculty."

Aaron nodded his head, his forehead glistening, and his face took on a resolute aspect. "We've got to move forward." His voice drifted slightly higher. "This is no time for the fainthearted."

Duxbury shot him a glance of mingled contempt, amusement and pity. But his face remained solemn.

"He's right. Let's have an open faculty meeting. We should invite Zo and the dean, but, as I've already said, we don't need to worry about Zo. And, I need hardly add, should I receive your support and be honored with the appointment, there will be an upward adjustment in your salaries."

Received in silence, the implicit bribe hung softly in the air. Junker's lip curled stiffly upward as he adjusted his tie. Boomer leaned back, smiling broadly, and scratched his ear. No one objected. A decision had been reached. By common agreement, Boomer was delegated responsibility for calling the meeting and making sure most members of the faculty would be present. Chairs scraped against the floor or furrowed the scanty carpet as they were pushed back. The group rose to depart. Leather wrinkled slowly into place on the couch as everyone but Duxbury filed from the room.

Duxbury also rose and shut a window, setting fast the rusted latch, then slumped in the chair behind his desk. He disliked the dean intensely. The man was too rumpled, too self-effacing and too principled. Largely unrecognized, the wellspring of his antipathy went deeper. Born Edward Elliott, he had been raised in Duxbury, Massachusetts, a town that became the origin of his nickname. Duxbury had graduated in precise, unbroken order from Milton Academy, Harvard College and Harvard Law School. Discovering early that the practice of law in a white shoe Boston law firm did not interest him, he attempted to secure a teaching position at a top-ranked law school, but the only institution to offer him a job was Crabshaw. And there he remained, despite efforts to transfer elsewhere. He had been deeply offended when Massoud

Ansari, another New Englander with credentials, so he thought, no better than his own, had been appointed dean.

It had been a tiring and tiresome meeting. Duxbury pinched the bridge of his elongated nose and then rested his crossed hands on the careless folds of his cardigan sweater while his graying head, balding in front, drooped forward. The little figurine remained, undisturbed, lying on its back at the rear of his desk. The room was silent, save for the ticking of a large, battered clock on the wall whose second hand jerked from marker to marker around the dial. It was only when the slanting rays of the sun illuminated Duxbury's face, an hour or so later, that he stirred. Rising stiffly, he bundled his willowy frame into a worn overcoat that had been hanging on a hook behind the door, placed a fur cap upon his head, grasped his invariable black umbrella with its shiny pearl handle, and departed his room, locking the door carefully behind him.

* * * * *

There was a dappling of snow that night, but the morning was bright and clear. It lacked the crystalline clarity of a day following a mid-winter storm, for the semester had progressed into early spring. There was a cheerful promise of warmth, a freshness in the air, that belied the thin, wet mantle of snow. Buds were near bursting on forsythia bushes, and an occasional crocus peeped through its white covering. It would not be long before the gray piles of snow vanished in icy rivulets.

Boomer was in a boisterous mood, and his bellowing mirth could be heard down the corridor. Cheerfully, he was fulfilling his appointed task, inviting his fellow faculty members to the meeting. Leaving one office, he knocked on Junker's door, then entered upon hearing an abrupt, gruff "come in".

Boomer turned around an armless, wooden chair before Junker's desk and straddled it, draping his massive, fleshy arms across its back.

"Great morning, isn't it. I don't care what it looks like out there, it finally feels like spring. It won't be long now."

Junker sat impassively, mustache at the ready.

Boomer continued: "Listen, a group of us got together yesterday. We all agreed. Given our present circumstances, we need to replace the dean. We'd like to have a meeting and talk about it and see how everyone feels. What do you think?"

One of Junker's eyebrows arched upward. His mustache twitched. Briefly, a puzzled expression crossed his features, quickly followed by a contemptuous glare.

"Idiot," he hissed. "Have you forgotten already that I was there? Sometimes I can't decide who are the biggest fools in this place – the students, the administration, or my faculty colleagues."

Chapter Eight

Janet Harborough

Janet Harbrough was working late. A secretary in the registrar's office and a part-time student in the university, she was a pretty young woman. She had to finish typing a term paper and so had decided to remain after working hours and use the computer in her office, two doors away from the dean's office at the end of the hall. No one in authority had told her, or others, of the possible burglary on the floor below hers. There were old, unreliable rumors, but there had been no repetition, and Janet dismissed them as idle chatter.

It was nearly dusk when the last of her co-workers quit for the day. "Don't stay too late now," the registrar said as she closed the door.

"I'll be leaving soon," Janet replied. "I've just a few more pages to type and some revisions." She could hear other doors closing, and footsteps receding down the corridor, and pretty soon she was alone in a cone of silence. No one else was on her floor, or most likely the floor beneath hers. Only the library remained open until eleven o'clock, and that was on the first floor.

After working for about an hour, she leaned back and read some of the pages she had typed. Then she rose and left the office to drink some water from a cooler near the stairwell at the end of the hallway. It was dark there, illuminated only by a single fluorescent light, and the quiet made her nervous. She drank and quickly returned. Soon, once again, only the sound of her fingers skipping over the keys of her computer echoed in the silence surrounding her.

By nine o'clock Janet was finished. She placed a neat stack of her typed pages in her book bag, put on a coat and shut the office door behind her. It was dark in the corridor, and her footfalls made a clicking sound on the linoleum floor as she walked toward the stairwell. She saw that someone had carelessly left on a lamp in the Admissions Office – something she had not noticed before – and its light shone dimly through a glass panel and under the door. It cast her elongated shadow against the opposite wall as, clutching her bag, she hurried along.

Did she hear a rustling noise from the same office? She was not sure, but it frightened her, and she walked faster. With some relief, she reached the stairwell and started to descend the stairs. She did not see or hear a man, a stocking mask pulled over his face, leave the Admissions Office and pad silently down the corridor after her.

Janet stopped at the foot of the stairs and slowly exhaled. She was only a few steps from the door to the outside where her car was parked when the man sprang down from the landing above her. He landed at her side in two quick bounds.

"Don't make a sound," he hissed.

Janet was aware that he was holding something in his hand, and with horror she realized it was a sharp-bladed hunting knife. He held it to her throat and ordered her outside.

"Move!" he hissed again as he forced her around to the dark side of the building away from the glare of lights illuminating the parking area just outside the door.

Not long thereafter two male students, having finished

their studies in the library, left the building by the same exit. They saw the contents of a book bag spilled onto the ground and heard a noise, difficult to identify, like soft moaning. Deciding to investigate, they rounded the corner and saw in the darkness two forms, one apparently grappling with the other.

"Hey!" one of them said. "Hey, hey. What's going on here?"

The attacker desisted and, only partially tumescent and with knife in hand, turned to the young men. "Get the hell out of here," he snarled.

He took a step forward, and Janet, freed from his indignities, ran around the two young men into the lighted parking area. She began to shriek for help. Her assailant, his prize having escaped, backed slowly away. The two young men were still staring at him dumbly as, smirking under his mask, he zipped his fly and then turned and ran into the darkness.

"Should we go after him?" one of the students asked the other.

"Are you kidding? With that knife? Let's see about the girl."

The two students retraced their steps and quickly found Janet sobbing by the side of her car. After conferring briefly, one of them ran into the building and alerted the librarian on duty. That person immediately called the police and then, reflecting on the matter, telephoned the dean.

"This better be important," the librarian heard Dean Ansari growl.

"Yes, sir, it is. We think a woman has just been raped by the side of the building."

"What?" There was a long pause, and the librarian heard the dean mutter, "Oh God, this is all we need." Then, in a firmer tone of voice, the dean asked: "Have you called the police?"

"Yes, sir."

"And... and does she need medical assistance?"

The librarian was flustered. "I didn't think of that. I'll do it right away. I think... I think I hear the police now."

"Good. I'm coming over. Give them all the cooperation you can. They may want to search the area, so keep onlookers away."

The librarian replaced the telephone and headed for the exit. Alerted by the noise, a few students who had been studying in the library began to peek out the windows and drift outside. The librarian made a futile effort to restrain them. He was soon aided by a police officer.

A patrol car, lights flashing, had pulled up next to Janet's car, and one of the officers spoke with her and the two male students. Another car arrived shortly thereafter, as did the dean. Curious student onlookers were barred from approaching the area where the crime occurred, and the dean entered the building with two officers to examine the offices and hallway on the floor where Janet had been working.

In the meantime, Janet was taken to the local hospital where she was examined for trauma and the presence of semen. By this time her hysteria had subsided. She was calm as she related to an attending officer all the details of the assault that she could recall. Unfortunately, she could not recall very much. She thought her assailant was probably a white male, above average in height, in his twenties and wearing dark clothing. She remembered seeing New Balance running shoes. And the knife; she remembered the knife. Above all, she remembered the terrifying, angry growl of his voice. It had been deep and husky but without an identifiable accent.

* * * * *

The next morning Dean Ansari was in his office when Lieutenant McCallister arrived. The detective was ushered promptly into the office and, after removing his coat and hat, sat in a proffered chair near to the couch. Looking straight at the dean, who had taken a seat near him, he shook his head slowly from side to side. "Well, Dean," he said, "it looks like you're running a crime factory here. What the hell is going on?"

The dean glanced at him bleakly. "I wish I knew. I really wish I knew. Thank God the young woman is all right... I mean, as all right as could be expected. We've given her a few days off, and if she needs more, she can have them." The dean frowned. "Have you spoken with her?"

"No, but Lieutenant Walsh is with her this morning trying to get some additional information. I've looked at her statement, and it doesn't look promising." Lieutenant McCallister leaned forward. "Have you any idea who might have done it? Anyone on the staff, a student, anyone who's visited the law school lately?"

"Not a clue."

"Have you any idea how the man gained access to this floor... or maybe elsewhere?"

"The dean shook his head. "Pretty much anyone can get into the building until around eight o'clock. We have security personnel who check every floor from time to time, and everyone knows to lock their office when they leave at night."

"From what the young woman said, we think he was in the Admissions Office," Lieutenant McCallister said. "How he got in, we don't know. It may have been a burglary – you know, steal a computer or something like that – and the rape was just a crime of opportunity."

"Could it be linked to the last time – you know, the time

when someone broke into one of our faculty offices, probably to steal something – or to the murder of Kevin?" the dean asked, his voice tense.

"Hard to say – the two break-ins are certainly similar, but compared to the homicide, they're a different kind of crime with a different weapon. We're not ruling out some sort of connection, but right now, we just don't know. I'll say this, though. It doesn't look good."

Glumly, the dean responded. "We're certainly having a harder time attracting students, and this will make the situation even worse. It's terrible. I've issued instructions to increase security, but we can't be everywhere."

Lieutenant McCallister picked up his coat and hat. "Right now I'd like to talk with members of your staff. Will that be a problem?"

"Not at all," Dean Ansari said, rising to his feet. "Not at all. I know we're in capable hands. I just hope to God we don't have a maniac loose in this place."

Chapter Nine

Zo Talks Tough

Lieutenant McCallister quietly shut the door to the dean's office, and the dean turned to a stack of letters and memoranda by the side of his desk. The mail flowed in, morning and afternoon, as if a spigot had been left carelessly open. With a muted sigh, he put down a note from the librarian, then picked up an announcement for a conference on products liability to be held in San Antonio. Nice place, San Antonio. Vaguely, he thought of the woman he had met there and almost taken to dinner. And then what might have happened? Middle-class virtue, in the usual forms of fear of social disapproval and disease, had won the day. To his lingering regret. Perfunctorily, he wrote a note across the top of the announcement, referring it to the professor teaching Torts.

Next in the pile was a memorandum. He had taken it in his hand when the light flashed on his telephone. Twice it blinked, then went steady when Mrs. Ackerman picked up the receiver in the outer office. There was a pause, and he just had time to glance at the page, noting that it was a request for some sort of meeting, when the buzzer for the intercom sounded.

"Dean Ansari, it's President Zo."

"Okay, Mrs. Ackerman. But screen any further calls and hold them up, because I'm reading this stack of mail."

He pressed the button for one of his extensions.

"Hi, Drew." He always called the president by his nickname. "I think I know why you called."

"You're damn right. What the hell is going on over there? A young woman raped right outside the building? I saw it in this morning's paper."

The dean slumped in his chair. "Yes," he said with a sigh. "It happened. We're taking steps to beef up security, and the police are already on it, looking for whoever did it."

"They damn well ought to be! This isn't going to improve the reputation of the school – or applications for admission."

"I know. You don't need to tell me.... I hope to God we find the perpetrator soon. That may explain Kevin Pannelli's murder, too."

There was a prolonged interval of silence. "Well," President Zo said, "that's one reason why I called. But first, have you seen the memorandum about the meeting?"

"No, but it's right here in front of me. I was just about to read it. What does it say?"

"Well, the first thing is what it doesn't say. It's a memo to the faculty calling for a meeting in a couple of weeks, but it doesn't come from anybody. You know: to – from. On this one, there's no 'from.'"

"What kind of meeting?" The dean was perplexed. Something did not seem right.

"It's the usual bravery of your so-called colleagues," President Zo responded caustically. "Or at least I assume it's from them. Take a look at it. They – I guess some of them – want a meeting to discuss replacing you as dean. It says applications are down, the bar-pass rate is down, and no heat is put on them to improve things. It seems to imply that it's your fault for not being demanding enough to make them demanding enough. Something like that."

Hastily, the dean read the memorandum while the president was speaking. Zo had the gist of it. The memorandum was either not well written or had been written to be deliberately vague. It called for a meeting of the faculty, and the president and vice presidents had been invited. So had he, probably because the author could think of no way to exclude him.

"Do you think we should take this seriously?" The dean was troubled. "Maybe it's some kind of weird joke from a couple of anonymous malcontents."

The president hesitated, then spoke firmly: "I don't think so. I think you've got to take this seriously. A couple of faculty members saw me this morning and said a meeting was in the works. They didn't say who was behind it, but they implied that most of the faculty will attend."

"This sure takes me by surprise."

"Me too. But don't get too worried about it. I mean, you can't help having it upset you, but don't blow it out of proportion. Sooner or later, faculties are always unhappy with deans."

"Well, sure, I suppose so."

"Anyway, this isn't really why I called you, although it was something we needed to talk about." President Zo paused and coughed. "Um,... when I came to work yesterday morning, I found a note taped to my office door. I was in a hurry and threw it on a stack of mail, and I didn't get to read it until the afternoon. It's very odd, maybe a threat of some sort – just one more strange thing around here – and I thought I should tell you about it. I turned it over to Lieutenant McCallister – and by the way, he's been to see me, but I assume you know that. Anyway, I kept a copy, and I'm wondering, I guess, if you know what it means."

The president stopped speaking. The dean waited silently for him to continue.

""It's kind of a rhyme, but not a very good one. I assume a student must have written it, perhaps as a prank, but... perhaps not. So... here it is:"

> There never were seven,
> But once there were six.
> Five was too many,
> Four's not a good mix.
> Three would be better,
> And better yet two.
> One will be left,
> And she will die too.

"What? And she will die too? Who will die too? Could you... could you read that again."

"It would probably be better if I sent you a copy – strictly confidential, of course. Any idea what it means?"

"I've no idea. It's strange... no, it's creepy. It makes me feel very uneasy, which is maybe what it's supposed to do. Is it some kind of sick joke?... No... no, it seems more like some kind of warning."

"You think a warning?"

"Yeah, that's what it seems like. But how do I know? What's the point of a warning when you don't even know what you're being warned about?"

"Maybe that's all the more reason why I'd better send you a copy. Maybe we're supposed to think about it... I agree with you. It's strange all right."

"No stranger than the meeting. Well, I take that back. It's stranger, but the meeting is pretty strange, too."

"Put worries out of your mind. I'm behind you one hundred percent. You're invulnerable as long as I back you up. I'll go to that meeting, and it'll be time for some tough talk. They'll be sorry they came."

The dean was relieved. "It's good to hear you say that," he said. "It makes a big difference... Now... if we could only figure out that sick note. Two students are dead, killed, maybe. It alludes to that... but it seems to be saying that more will die. Meeting or no meeting, Drew, that kind of publicity will sink the school for good."

"Possibly... yes, possibly," the president responded, slowly. "But that's why we've got to figure it out and trust that the police are going to get to the bottom of this mess. In the meantime... Yes, yes," the dean heard him say, "the door's open... come in." The conversation stopped. President Zo appeared to have cupped his hand over the receiver, but the dean nevertheless heard his muffled comment, in response to an inquiry, "We're talking about it right now." There was more inaudible conversation, followed by the removal of his hand. "Allison just came in," he said. "I told her about the note a few minutes ago – just before I called you." His voice grew slightly fainter, but it was loud enough for the dean to hear. "I can't carry on two conversations at once. Here, you talk to him directly." Then, much louder: "Allison wants to talk with you. I'll get back on in a minute."

Allison Fetherheft was an extraordinarily obese woman. She had a well-deserved reputation for getting things done, no matter the personal cost. She cowed any opposition, and neither tact nor deftness were in her repertoire. Her responsibilities were many, including oversight of the university's Accounting Office.

Fetherheft spoke: "I've just heard about this poem. What're you doing about solving the murder – or should I say these murders? And the rape?"

"What do you mean, what am I doing about them? I'm not the police. That's their job."

"You're the dean, and it happened in your school." Her voice was a finely calibrated mixture of menace and loathing. "I trust that I don't have to remind you that three people work in the Accounting Office, and I'm their superior. It certainly seems likely that I'm the one' who's going to die too." Her tone had become shrill. "So get cracking."

"Well, I'm not so sure about that," the dean answered. "What makes you think… what makes you think the note is referring to the Accounting Office?"

There was no response. He heard the telephone being fumbled, and President Zo's reassuring voice broke in. "Don't get alarmed. Allison is a little upset, perhaps understandably, but it seems premature to be trying to interpret what that note is saying… if it isn't just a cruel joke."

"It sure is premature," the dean said, "and even if she's right, I don't think there's much that I can do about it. I hope you can calm her down."

"Of course I can. We'll get to the bottom of it… and while I've got you on the phone and we're on this general subject, what do you hear from the police? There's no word here, but I assume they're keeping in touch with you."

"More or less," the dean answered. " I contacted Lieutenant McAllister a couple of days ago. He tells me they've talked to most of our faculty, some of the staff and even a few students. And of course they've searched the place. But so far they haven't come up with much. It's pretty discouraging."

"Do they have anything to go on at all?"

"I'm sure they don't tell me everything. But as far as I can tell, it's a dry hole… I mean, no real clues."

"That's discouraging. We absolutely have to… we must… put this matter behind us." President Zo sighed, then changed the subject. "Well, now, about that meeting," his voice rose with optimism, "we're going to make some changes, get applications up, and in a few months the law school will be a different place. For the time being, try to relax. This is a piece of cake compared to being bounced around in a field ambulance with half your leg blown off."

President Zo laughed. He liked making references to the time years before when, as a young Marine second lieutenant, he had fought, and then been wounded, in the Korean War. His practiced listeners were never sure how much truth there was in his stories, particularly as they seemed to change from time to time and occasionally contradict each other. But there seemed little doubt that he had been in Korea, although one of his childhood friends, visiting the university, had implied that the injury to his leg was the result of a schoolyard accident.

Chapter Ten

Prigley Stirs the Pot

Mrs. Ackerman sat in a stiff-backed, wooden chair on the other side of the dean's wide desk. She had set her dictation pad and pen to one side while he riffled through a stack of recently typed memoranda and letters. This ritual occurred at least every other day. Her work was undergoing inspection: a neverending process. Approval was conferred by a scrawled initial on a memorandum or a signature at the foot of a letter. Lack of approval occurred whenever he corrected a typographical error or changed a sentence not to his liking.

Mrs. Ackerman guarded the dean, his office and his schedule with a strong maternal instinct. Intellectual acuity, as far as he could tell, eluded her, but she had a zealous desire to please; she also typed well, and she found it trying to have her work so closely scrutinized, particularly as she was never confident she had properly transcribed his sometimes garbled mumblings from the disc he handed her each morning.

He was affixing initials and signatures, however, with regularity. Then, as was almost always the case, he paused.

"No, no," he muttered. Then: "Mrs. Ackerman, it says here in this letter that the position I espouse will only be rejected by those who are 'uniformed.' I suppose that means it will be accepted by those in mufti?"

"That's the way you dictated it," she said, reading reproof in his furrowed brow as he reread the offending passage.

From prior, frustrating experience, the dean knew better than to argue, and he immediately regretted his snide comment. Nonetheless, to protect himself, he suggested that he could not possibly have dictated the sentence as written, because it was not consonant with his thinking.

"The word has to be 'uninformed,'" he said, making the correction in ink.

The dean handed the page to Mrs. Ackerman, who glanced reproachfully at him and then scrutinized the change carefully. He was, of course, correct. So why did he feel he'd been wrong? He returned to perusing the documents before him, then looked up.

"I think there's too much that's very odd going on," he said.

"Oh, that poor Kevin Pannelli. Such a nice young man. And still no one seems to know why it happened or who did such a dreadful thing. One of the students in here yesterday said that he can't even go into that bathroom anymore. And then that lovely young woman, Janet, almost next door. How could such a thing have happened?"

"I wasn't... " The dean checked himself. He did not want to enter into a discussion about the investigatory frailties of the police department, a matter about which Mrs. Ackerman claimed unaccountable expertise. "I was referring to this meeting that's been called. Isn't it odd that everyone seems to be taking it seriously, and no one even knows who called it. To me that's very strange."

He initialed the paper before him, then the next one.

"Every place where I've ever worked has been strange," Mrs. Ackerman said, concern on her care-worn features. "Perhaps," she ventured, after a moment's hesitation, "if it's declining applications for admission that's the problem, we could attract students from Central America. Everyone seems to be leaving there these days."

"Mrs. Ackerman, what makes you think they want to be lawyers? Anyway, most of them aren't college graduates."

"But I'm sure they're very nice people."

"What's that got to do with it?"

"Well, you're always talking about ethics in the profession, so I would think it has a great deal to do with it."

Aware that he was a man sinking into unknown depths, the dean wisely refrained from responding. Mrs. Ackerman was about to continue when the telephone rang. After a moment's hesitation, she reached across the desk and, with some effort, even though the dean pushed the telephone toward her, picked up the receiver.

"Dean Ansari's office... I'm sorry, he's in a meeting... " Her guardian instinct surfaced. There was audible comment at the other end, delivered with urgency. "Let me see," Mrs. Ackerman said cautiously, "perhaps I can interrupt him."

Pressing the hold button, she said, "It's one of our students, and she seems to be extremely upset about something. Do you want to speak with her?"

"Who is it?"

"Ruth Dinsmore."

The dean grimaced. Glancing down at his desk, he exhaled slowly and audibly. If the telephone call had been from any other student, he would have referred it to the associate dean, but Ruth Dinsmore was a student member of the Financial Aid Committee and the head of the Women's Association.

"All right," he said, "I'll talk to her. Put her on."

Mrs. Ackerman took the call off hold. "The dean can speak with you now. Just a moment."

She handed him the receiver.

"Hi, Ms. Dinsmore, what can I do for you?" He attempted a tone of affability.

"Do for me? I'll tell you what you can do for me!"

It was an inauspicious beginning. Making another wry face, the dean held the receiver a couple of inches from his ear. In consequence, Mrs. Ackerman became an unintended, but not unwilling, eavesdropper to the conversation.

"What seems to be the trouble?"

"Seems?" She spat the word through the telephone wires. "You've got a big problem on your hands."

Yes, I do, he thought.

"I'm calling from the office of the Women's Association," Ms. Dinsmore continued. "And one of our fu..." Uncharacteristically, she checked herself in a surprising gesture of gentility. "I mean, one of our really cute male students – I mean, really, really cute – just called us."

"How do you know it was one of our students? Did he identify himself?"

"No. But I'd know the voice of Prigley Sassoon anywhere. I sat near him in class. That damn, heavy, hick accent is a dead giveaway."

Oh God. Not Prigley. What's he done this time? "Well," said the dean, "if it was Prigley, and I don't know how we prove it... someone could have been imitating him, you know. But if it was Prigley, what did he do?"

But of course it was Prigley. He knew it full well. That rascal could not resist tweaking Ms. Dinsmore. It was in character – his character: the dean's problem.

"You don't have to worry, Dean Ansari. Just ask him. He won't deny it. He probably thinks he was being funny."

"Go on. Let's hear it."

"I was sitting here, minding my own business and doing some reading – I'd just finished writing some letters for our Women in the Law Conference – when the telephone rang. When I picked it up, this man said, 'Is this the Women's Association office?' or something like that. And when I said it was – and by this time I was already sure it was Prigley Sassoon – he asked if he could send over some laundry to be done. And when I told him – nicely, too – that he must have the wrong number, he said, 'No, not if it's the Women's Association office.' And then he said his boxer shorts needed mending. I started to really get angry, and just as polite as could be, he said, 'Oh, and by the way, bake me up some cookies and send them back with the laundry.' That's a fair quote. And he hung up. And of course I didn't know where he called from. I was pretty mad. I looked up his home number and called, but there was no answer. So I called you."

Dean Ansari emitted a muted sigh when she stopped speaking. He strongly supported women's rights, but it was hard to appreciate Ms. Dinsmore's drill sergeant stridency. It was equally hard to dislike Prigley.

"I'll ask him to come in," he said, "and try to get to the bottom of this."

"All right, Dean Ansari. Please do that. I think he should be disciplined. The women are frightened enough after what happened to Janet Harbrough. We don't need harassment on top of it." There was a pause. "It's not fair."

The tone of the last words took the dean by surprise. She sounded hurt. He said, "Don't worry. We'll take care of it. At the least, he owes you an apology. I think you should come in, too. We need to talk it out."

Ms. Dinsmore agreed, her voice slightly tremulous, and the conversation ended. The dean replaced the receiver.

Mrs. Ackerman was smiling. "I couldn't help hearing," she said. "Honestly, you get more crazy problems. Sometimes I don't know how you stand it."

"That makes two of us. But we've got to get him in here. Please leave a message on the student bulletin board for him to come by for an appointment."

Mrs. Ackerman made a note in her pad. When she raised her eyes, the dean had already begun to leaf through the remaining papers in the pile before him, but he had lost his concentration.

"This is all we need," he said. "I really get tired of dealing with stupid problems like this."

Mrs. Ackerman, who had long since become his confidante, nodded sympathetically. "I'm sure Kevin's murder and that horrible rape must weigh terribly on your mind. And, of course, if applications were up, I think you'd feel a good deal better."

For a few moments, there was silence.

"It's the police who have to deal with those crimes," he responded finally. "Damn it, I wish they'd get on with it.... And as for applications, I've run out of ideas. I really don't know what to do."

* * * * *

Two days later, almost to the hour, Mrs. Ackerman ushered Prigley into the dean's office – without the usual fanfare and hint of trumpets – and he sat, looking sheepish, at one end of the ample couch. His greeting at the door with the dean had been cordial, if slightly restrained, but now the room was quiet. The dean stood by the window, gazing out. There was a hint of spring, an ephemeral suggestion of green, in the trees flanking the walk into the building. It will not be long, he thought, until another academic year is at an end. Both men were awaiting the arrival of Ruth Dinsmore.

Prigley was no stranger to the dean's office. Indeed, he had been there only days before Kevin Pannelli's death, attempting to explain a recent escapade; returning to discuss the matter further, he had been interrupted by the arrival of His Jollity and Mattress Head. This unresolved issue, by itself, created a lingering mood of tension between them. However, there had been other instances, too many other instances, when Prigley had been fetched before the dean as a miscreant.

The problem was not ability. He was an excellent student, with high grades. Nor was it an unwillingness to abide by academic and administrative standards. Rather, it was that he liked pranks; he simply could not resist them. He also liked life; he enjoyed drinking beer with his friends, telling jokes and dating the prettiest members of the female half of the student body. His laughter was infectious. Not surprisingly, he was very well liked by the faculty and staff as well as by his fellow students.

However, it was one thing to like women – and of that, in his case, there was no doubt – and it was another to take on the Women's Association. To some of its members, Prigley was atavistic. He was not funny. He was just the sort of cheerful, unconsciously self-assertive male that the more militant members had been born to stamp out. And now he had done the unthinkable; he had actually challenged the gravity of their mission.

It was not, in fact, that Prigley disagreed with that mission. Basically, he supported it in an idealized, unthinking sort of way, easily perceiving the justice of equality. But browsing in the pleasures and challenges of his vigorous, young life, he was not given to causes and crusades. To the contrary, his enjoyment came from poking fun at those whose earnestness was unleavened by any sense of humor about the intrinsic absurdity of the human condition.

When Prigley learned the reason for his most recent summons to the dean's office, he had gotten serious – and nervous – about the possibility of another disciplinary notation in his student file. Perhaps, he reflected, the sheer volume would reflect adversely on him in any fitness report to the bar examiners. Arising in his apartment that morning, therefore, he had carefully shaved and showered. The product of a West Virginia family of modest means, he ignored his usual mode of dress in favor of a pair of green chino slacks, scruffy loafers (his only pair of leather shoes), a yellow, button-down shirt caught at the neck by a wide, aqua-marine tie on which was painted a leaping deer, and a blue, checkered tweed jacket. Predictably, the result was hideous, but his pleasure in his garish attire was enough to disarm all but the most severe Ivy League critic. If looks could carry the day, Prigley was confident of a favorable outcome.

Ruth Dinsmore, on the other hand, knew how to dress properly. The daughter of a wealthy businessman, a man who had prospered in the export-import trade in Kansas City, she had attended a correct, socially acceptable country day school, graduated from Miss Porter's, and then matriculated at Bennington. Given wealth and advantage, she easily measured their worth. From her father she learned two things: a sense that she could succeed, regardless of gender, and a dislike of his pushy materialism. From her maternal side, she acquired a beautiful face and figure that she was usually at pains to disguise lest she be like her mother, who was a vacuous, babbling socialite with neither intellectual pretensions nor ability.

In college Ruth had found in the women's movement a way to express and reconcile these different aspects of herself. Eschewing social positioning, she had gravitated toward debate and activism on behalf of women's issues. She marched holding placards, wrote letters to her Congressperson and state legislators, and prepared for a career in law where her idealism might find practical expression. She also adopted baggy pants and sweatshirts, went without makeup and tied her long hair back in a severe knot to disguise her obvious femininity. And then, as a capstone, she chose Crabshaw, a place so relentlessly drab that it shone, albeit guilelessly, as a counter-culture icon.

But today was different. Today she had to prevail over a happy-go-lucky hayseed, a young man who, by his speech and deportment, represented the apotheosis of the enemy. Ruth was determined that he should be disciplined, and she bent her formidable intelligence toward that goal.

She also, like Prigley, had risen early. She also considered her attire, and, in order to make the best possible impression on the dean, who was known to admire women, she selected a plain blue dress, cut with restrained good taste, and low-heeled pumps. After glancing at herself while she turned several times before a long mirror in her bedroom, she let fall her waving, chestnut hair and applied a hint of pale lipstick. A modest gold pin affixed below her left shoulder completed her ensemble. The result was striking: a stunningly beautiful young woman.

Thus attired, Ruth entered the dean's outer office, her beige raincoat slung gracefully over one arm. Mrs. Ackerman was at her post. When the door opened, she glanced up at the intrusion, then returned to her computer. But a thought had been born, and it started to itch. In two or three seconds, she looked up again.

"Why Ms. Dinsmore, I scarcely recognized you." She removed her fingers from the keyboard. "Don't you look nice today."

Ruth smiled. She had already appraised her appearance, but it was good to have even tactless corroboration. "I'm here to see the dean about a personal matter," she said. "I have an appointment."

After knocking gently on his door, Mrs. Ackerman opened it slightly and said, "Dean Ansari, Ruth Dinsmore is here to see you."

"Ask her to come in."

Mrs. Ackerman swung wide the door, and Ruth walked by her into the office.

There was a moment of awkward silence while the older and younger man attempted to adjust to a perception so different from their expectations. The dean had been standing by the window, and he ambled forward, holding out his hand. Prigley, who had been sitting on the couch, rose to his feet, a confused gape on his features.

Her trim figure erect, and her turquoise eyes looking openly into his own, Ruth took the dean's outstretched hand.

"Won't you sit down," he said.

She chose the opposite end of the couch from Prigley. As was his custom, the dean slouched into a wooden chair at one side of the coffee table, declining to sit authoritatively behind his desk.

"Well," he said, "tell me again what's going on." He cleared his throat and drummed his fingers on his knees.

Ruth glanced quickly at Prigley, who was staring pointedly at the floor, and told her story again. Nearing the end, she concluded: "And then this voice said 'put some cookies in the laundry when you return it' or something like that. Then he hung up."

"Are you sure it was Prigley?"

"Why don't you ask him?"

"All right." The dean looked squarely at Prigley, who had baffled puzzlement on his features. "Was it you?"

"Well, you see, I was just… I mean… yes, sir, it was."

Prigley had obviously erred. Like the dean, all he had seen was a bespectacled caterpillar, and he had not had the inclination or wit to recognize that a beautiful butterfly might emerge from its chrysalis. He shifted uncomfortably in his seat as he spoke. The result was a jumble of disingenuous calculation, betrayed by stumbling speech. He tried with haphazard effectiveness to modify his West Virginia accent in order to make a better impression. Not on the dean, which had been his goal upon entering the office. On Ruth.

Gruffly, the dean queried: "Can you tell us why you did it?"

"Well, sir, I… I thought I was bein' funny. Like, you know, just havin' a good time." He hesitated. Ruth Dinsmore was surveying him with a fixed, steady expression. "I mean… thinking about it… I'd have to say that, uh, it was a pretty… well, not such a… I mean, you know, a dumb thing to do."

"What do you think we ought to do about it?" The dean was perplexed. Was this faltering student before him a new Prigley? It was certainly not the self-assured, easy-going young man with whom he had had dealings in the past.

Ruth offered an answer. "There is no question that he must be disciplined. What he did will undoubtedly get out to the rest of the student body." She looked at the dean sharply to make sure he got the point: no *in camera* proceedings here, and be so advised. "It's unconscionable to have rudeness between fellow students when they're going about their legitimate business. All sense of morale and school spirit – I might even say harmony – breaks down. I don't need to remind you that we've got lots of different clubs at Crabshaw: clubs for young Republicans, for African Americans, for our Jewish students, for people interested in international law and the environment. And we also have a Women's Association. Students have a right to associate and pursue their interests as long as they don't break the law. That's a First Amendment right. Women are no different. We have a perfect right to get together to discuss women's issues and work for them without being insulted."

It was a good speech, thought through as she walked to the school that morning. It had been delivered well, with firm resolution and conviction. The steel in her voice was vintage Ruth Dinsmore. There was only one problem: steel was not needed. Prigley was not fighting back, nor was he trying to smile and genially manipulate the outcome. He simply stared, looking faintly woebegone.

The dean looked keenly from one to the other, not sure what to do.

After a pause, Prigley spoke. "I, ah... Ruth... look, truly, I'm sorry. I really am. I sure hope you'll forgive me."

His words also were delivered with conviction, although uttered with a totally different demeanor than usual. He sounded contrite.

Ruth shifted her position on the couch, turning so that she faced Prigley and not the dean. She looked at him quizzically. She had come to exact vengeance, and to fight for it, but it was clear that she had already won. No fool, she could not ignore the look of frank admiration in Prigley's eyes.

With some difficulty, she shifted her gaze to the dean, who broke the charged silence. "Let me repeat. What do you think we ought to do about it? I know students, and student organizations, have rights. I'm prepared to uphold them."

"Maybe we don't need to let this get out to the student body," Ruth answered. "Perhaps we can find some solution which upholds our rights, and also see that Mr. Sass... I mean, Prigley, does not do this kind of thing again." Her tone still had a flinty edge, as if a third grade teacher were admonishing an errant pupil.

Prigley's face brightened. "I know," he said. "You don't let men in the Women's Association, do you? Oh... that was dumb. Of course not... me again." He was stumbling. "What I wanted to say was that I could, if you let me, do some work for the association... I mean, I could work with you, Ruth. Maybe you need someone to tack up posters or type letters or something like that. I'd be willing as a way to show I'm sorry."

His remarks were delivered haltingly, but with evident sincerity. The dean turned to Ruth. "What do you think?" The irony of Prigley tacking up posters for the Women's Association was not lost on him. Perhaps he would learn something. It did not escape him, however, that Prigley had devised a clever way to achieve penance through good works yet be with a beautiful law student. His ingenuity never ceased to surprise.

Neither, the dean could see, did the suggestion, with all its possibilities, escape the discernment of Ruth Dinsmore.

"I'd like to think it over," she responded. "The idea does make some sense, but I'm not sure the other officers will agree. We've never had a male law student do work for us before, and some people will be pretty surprised if the first one is Prigley Sassoon – particularly if I don't tell them the reason why."

She had started these remarks looking at the dean, but she ended them looking directly at Prigley. What a strangely dressed creature, she thought, yet good looking and with virtually limitless possibilities for improvement. Not that too much improvement would be desirable. Prigley was unselfconsciously out of step, and that very quality appealed to her streak of rebellion.

"There's no reason why you shouldn't tell the other officers," the dean said. Both students broke their unintended, mutual trance. "On the other hand, maybe it wouldn't be such a good idea. Maybe the others wouldn't feel good knowing that his work for you had been ordered by me as punishment."

"Oh no, sir," Prigley broke in. "Not punishment. Not punishment at all. I'm doin' it 'cause I want to."

"Well, whatever you say. I'm not concerned about the label. The point is that, instead of a disciplinary notation in your student file, you have volunteered to do free work for the Women's Association." The dean paused, then added, looking at Ruth, "Ms. Dinsmore, you will be responsible for making sure the work is done. It will be for free, and I think five hours or so a week for the remainder of the semester sounds about right. Let's see… that should, I think, come to about thirty hours."

"I have to think it over," Ruth said again, still suspicious. "But I suppose it will work." Unblinking, she looked at Prigley.

"It has to. Otherwise, I've got to think of something else. You two work it out and let me know what you come up with.

And Ms. Dinsmore, if there's any backsliding, I want to be told."

Prigley rose, a smile wreathing his features. "Thanks, Dean Ansari. You won't be disappointed in me."

"I hope not."

Prigley turned to Ruth, who was also rising to depart. "Would you like to have a cup of coffee with me? We can talk over what it is you'd like for me to do."

"All right, I guess." She hesitated, her face puckered by a frown. "But I have class in half an hour. We'll have to cross the street." Her voice was crisp but not unfriendly.

The dean extended his hand, first to Ruth and then to Prigley. Ruth spoke: "Thank you, Dean Ansari. I guess – I hope – we've disposed of this matter fairly." She gave him a dazzling smile. Erect and slender, she walked out of the office, followed by her chastened, yet eager, former adversary.

The dean watched them go. I'd no idea Ruth Dinsmore was so beautiful, he thought, or that, seemingly, she and Prigley might like each other. But she'd better keep an eye on him.

Mrs. Ackerman appeared at the door. "My, those two certainly left with smiles on their faces. They looked like they were heading off somewhere together. What did you do?"

"Not much, actually. I thought it would be a difficult meeting, as you know."

"And it wasn't?"

"No. Prigley came up with a good suggestion that solved everything." The dean laughed. "It also gave him a way to get to know her better."

"What was it?"

"Working for the Women's Association. For Ruth."

"Him?"

"Yes."

"It figures. I wouldn't put anything past that young man. It would even be like him to have set up this situation just to get to know her better. Still, if anyone can keep him in line, I'll bet she can."

"I hope he takes his eyes off her. She was surprisingly attractive today, wasn't she?"

"She certainly was. Not the Ruth Dinsmore we usually see. No wonder it turned his head around."

New Developments

Chapter Eleven

The Meeting

Prigley honored his word. Not, given his motives, that there could have been any doubt. Two days after his meeting with Ruth and the dean – and the brief interlude following that meeting when he joined Ruth in the coffee shop – he went to the Women's Association office and accepted his first assignment: typing addresses on envelopes. No chore too menial in a worthy cause!

Ruth reported these developments by leaving a note with a distracted Mrs. Ackerman, who conveyed it to the dean along with the inevitable stack of morning mail.

The dean was also distracted, but he read the note with wry amusement. The day of the meeting had arrived. He knew that it was important, but there had been no prior discussion. Normally, he set the agenda for meetings. Not knowing who had called this one, he did not know whom to ask about it. Nor did he wish to appear anxious or insecure by making other than casual inquiries, which had produced no result.

In mid-afternoon, a puzzled frown upon his face, he set off for the conference room in the central administration building of the university. The main campus of Heidelschmidt University was on the other side of town, several blocks from the law school. Once on the edge of urban development, it had long since been swallowed by metropolitan clutter. Its leafy, tree-lined walks and stolid brick buildings were an oasis in a decaying, mixed residential and commercial neighborhood.

The name of the university sprang from two sources. Its first, principal benefactor, Alonzo Schmidt, had been a student in Germany for two years after obtaining a local degree in engineering. Smitten by his experiences in the land of his forefathers, Mr. Schmidt had built the university's first classroom building and endowed its first professorship, the Alonzo Schmidt Chair in Germanic Languages, from wealth derived from a brewery founded by his father. Mr. Schmidt wanted to duplicate Heidelberg University in the far reaches of the American Midwest. This noble instinct, however, warred with his thirst for recognition and immortality. Thus was born a compromise: Heidelschmidt University, or Old Heidelschmidt, as it was known to its students and graduates.

Shortly after the founding of the university, the Board of Trustees had the opportunity, at nominal cost, to purchase a struggling, proprietary law school. A few years earlier, a Mr. Crabshaw had donated a building to this law school – a renovated brassiere factory – which was not far from the courthouse, city hall and downtown law offices. In gratitude, the law school had adopted the Crabshaw name. Crabshaw School of the Law became the first graduate program of the fledgling university, and for many years it provided a tidy sum of extra income for other departments. Only recently, with declining applications, had its finances become a problem.

The walk across town was not arduous, although it took nearly half an hour. The dean could have saved time by taking a trolley, its rails cut into asphalt and cobblestone streets bounded by a jumble of storefronts, but the day was warm. Crocuses and forsythia had given way to budding tulip trees.

There was a zest of renewed life in the air, and he wanted to experience it. Added to his enjoyment of nature was the sense that another difficult academic year was drawing to a close. Classes would end soon, and graduation was only a few weeks away.

He entered the university's main gate. On one side there was the noisy bustle of a commercial world; on the other, quiet contemplation. Rounding a corner on the brick walk before the administration building, the dean encountered – indeed, nearly bumped into – Duxbury.

Startled, he said, "Why, hello Duxbury. I didn't know you were coming to this meeting."

Too late he realized his mistake. Most nicknames were known, and they were occasionally used in derision or affection behind the backs of their possessors. But they were seldom used face to face. A breach of etiquette had occurred.

Duxbury, however, responded with aplomb. "Hello, Badger, it's so good to see you." He grinned at his riposte. The dean wasn't fond of his nickname, and people knew it. "I didn't know you were coming either," he continued. "Let's go in and see what the fuss is all about."

Together, they entered the building – Duxbury, tolerant, forgiving, chatting amiably; the dean, laughing nervously and a trifle loudly, anxious to make amends. The building was different from those surrounding it, built of limestone and not red brick, as befitted the central hub of the university. Its columned portico was wreathed in ivy. A seated statue of Alonzo Schmidt, on a suitably high pedestal, had been erected a few paces before the steps leading to the entrance. He gazed out upon his creation, severe but benign, a jowly face (his brow glazed with pigeon droppings) set squarely atop an antique collar, flowing tie and morning coat. Inscribed on the pedestal on a copper plaque, greened and weathered with age, were the words "Alonzo Schmidt, Our Benefactor and Founder, 1832-1903."

Inside, two opposed, curving staircases, with ornate banisters and railings, led upward from a small, marble foyer. Over the stairwell in the center of the upstairs hallway were two imposing oak doors flanked by portraits of former presidents. Behind the doors was the conference room, a large, paneled chamber with a long table in the middle illuminated by two hanging chandeliers. More portraits – in this case of former chairmen of the Board – graced the walls. Two latticed windows, nearly floor to ceiling in height and bounded by severely creased draperies, permitted extra light.

The faculty normally met within the law school, but large meetings with the president were always conducted in the conference room. So were meetings of the Board of Trustees. President Zo was, as usual, seated at the head of the table, and most of the faculty had already arrived. Mattress Head was there, and Bathroom Bob, and Junker and The Duchess. Aaron, His Jollity and Windy Dave were at the opposite end of the table from the president.

Lieutenant McCallister was seated to the immediate right of the president. Also at the meeting, somewhat to the dean's surprise, were the two university vice presidents. They sat near the president. One, Tony Caribe, was in charge of budget and finance, with the exception of student accounts. Short, thin and humorless, with piercing black eyes, narrow lips and nose, he was, as usual, fidgeting with papers on the table before him. The other, Allison Fetherheft, who was also provost, reclined back in her chair, a mound of gelatinous malevolence, surveying each faculty member in turn through squinty, close-set eyes. The skin on her forearms, folded truculently across her chest, was the color of plucked chicken.

Duxbury and the dean parted upon entering the room and took available seats around the table. Noting their arrival, President Zo rapped on the table, and the murmur of noise within the room subsided.

"We are gathered here," he began portentously, "at what I take to be the request of the faculty as a whole, no single person having convened the meeting." He looked around the room, and aside from a few baffled faces, there was no sign of disagreement. "In view of the fact that I was invited to attend, it seemed to me best that we hold the meeting here. And so I asked you to come to the conference room."

No one had suspected that the meeting would be held anywhere else. The president rarely came to the law school, which was, typically, almost alien territory within the university.

President Zo continued: "Before we get to the matter at hand, however, I've asked Lieutenant McCallister of our local Police Department to join us and give us a report on the recent, unhappy events at the law school." He turned to Lieutenant McCallister. "Antwan, I'm going to turn the meeting over to you for a few minutes."

Lieutenant McCallister pushed back his chair and rose to his feet. "Thank you, President Zo. I'll be brief, as there's not much to say. And I'll be glad to answer questions." He spoke well and easily, only betraying nervousness by occasionally checking the knot in his tie. "As you know, one of your students, Kevin Pannelli, was killed not long ago in a bathroom in the basement of the law school. While we are still searching for clues and don't know all the facts, there seems little doubt it was a murder, or at a minimum manslaughter. Another student, Thomas Headly, died two days previous to Kevin under suspicious circumstances. We are now treating his death also as a homicide.

"In addition," Lieutenant McCallister cleared his throat, "a staff member in your Registrar's Office was sexually assaulted just outside the school on school premises. This crime and the deaths of Kevin Pannelli and Thomas Headly may or may not be related to each other. The homicides apparently occurred in different ways, and we're still pretty much in the dark as to the exact manner or motive. Rape, of course, is an altogether different criminal act. So far we have very little evidence as to who might be the perpetrator, or perpetrators, of these crimes. We've thoroughly inspected the locus of each offense and have spoken to many people – and, incidentally, I'd like to thank most of you for taking the time to speak with my associate, Lieutenant Walsh, and me."

A professor raised his hand and asked: "Are there any possible suspects, any at all?"

"No," the lieutenant answered. "We have some theories, but nowhere near enough evidence to file charges. So right now we can't rule out anyone. Everyone is under suspicion."

"But we're lawyers, not criminals," another faculty member said.

Vice President Caribe smiled frostily. In an audible whisper to the person seated next to him, he said, "What's the difference?"

A female member of the faculty spoke without being called upon. "There are rumors that someone broke into one of our offices at night. Can you tell us anything about that?"

"No, I can't. It's a low level crime. One of your students may have been trying to purloin a paper or change his or her grade. If you have any idea who it was, or why that person was there, please let me or my associate know."

Lieutenant McCallister looked around the room, but there was no rejoinder. He resumed speaking. "One interesting thing has happened recently which may give us an opening. Your president received a poem that was taped to his door and later turned over to me. I'd like to read it to you." He removed a slip of paper from the inside pocket of his jacket, then fished reading glasses from the breast pocket of his suit and adjusted them on his nose. He began:

> There never were seven,
> But once there were six.
> Five was too many,
> Four's not a good mix.
> Three would be better,
> And better yet two.
> One will be left,
> And she will die too.

"If any of you know what this means, or can figure it out," Lieutenant McCallister said, "we need to hear from you. Dean Ansari knows how to reach me, but just in case, this is my number." He stated, then repeated his telephone number slowly. Several of those present wrote it down.

"Who's it referring to?" one faculty member asked nervously. "Could it be members of the faculty?"

"We just don't know," the lieutenant answered. "At this point, it could be referring to almost anyone."

A ripple of anxiety circled the room, accompanied by several murmured comments: Are we in danger walking to class? Perhaps every faculty member should be assigned a security guard. Would it be a good idea to close the school and reopen in the fall?

Timorously, Aaron raised his hand, his fingers twitching for recognition, and President Zo acknowledged him. "If we're in danger," he said, "and I think we may be, then I move that every member of the faculty be issued a bulletproof vest."

His motion was immediately seconded.

Fetherheft glared at him. "Aren't you leaving out the staff? We're just as important to the university as you are."

Vice President Caribe turned to face Zo with a pained expression on his face. "The cost," he rasped. "Does anyone have any idea what these vests will cost?"

"Okay," Aaron said. "I'll withdraw my motion with permission of the second and substitute another. We'll just have to exercise some triage. All senior members of the faculty and staff will get bulletproof vests. Junior faculty can be placed on a waiting list."

"And other members of the staff?" someone asked.

"They can be given whistles."

"Police whistles don't come cheap," Vice President Caribe said through clenched teeth.

"They don't have to be fancy," another faculty member volunteered. "Plastic whistles ought to do, and the university might get a discount by buying them in bulk."

Vice President Caribe rolled his eyes.

"What about the students?" The Duchess asked.

Several faculty members stared at her with blank

expressions, uncomprehending. "Oh, them," one mumbled. "Well, they'll just have to hoof it on their own."

Lieutenant McCallister broke into the discussion. "It's probably not my place to speak," he said, "but I think you're blowing this way out of proportion. After all, it was students and a staff member, not professors, who were attacked. And none of these crimes involved a gun, as far as we know. Sensible vigilance – keeping your eyes and ears open – is your best defense."

"Lieutenant McCallister is absolutely right," President Zo said. "Unless I hear an objection, we should table the motion and get on with the main purpose of this meeting."

Lieutenant McCallister removed his glasses, then rose to go. Replacing the paper on which the poem was written in his inside jacket pocket, he nodded to the president and faculty.

"Antwan," the president said, "many thanks for coming. We'll no doubt be in touch." The room was silent as President Zo waited patiently for the lieutenant to leave the room.

"Now – as I understand it," he said as the door closed, "there's a feeling of discontent within the law faculty, or at least some significant portion of the faculty, about the current status of the law school. Your bar pass rate is down. As a result, it seems, so are your applications. A decline in applications means a decline in enrollment and revenue."

Vice President Caribe nodded his head in agreement.

"Some of you are asking what we can do to reverse this situation. I share your concern. Jobs may be at stake. Some of you are even asking whether the school is getting the most effective leadership at this critical point in its history."

This is it, the dean thought. Now he lays it on the line. Tough talk will end this mutiny, if it is one.

But the president continued in a different vein. "I think first that we should set out some ground rules. We're all friends here, and we're speaking candidly to each other. This meeting has been called for a frank exchange of views. And something else. This is an educational institution that is striving for excellence. We can only grow great by striving greatly."

He mouthed this cliche without a flicker of embarrassment or hesitation, then glanced around the room.

Aaron's hand was in the air again. Zo acknowledged its presence.

"I think," Aaron piped in his earnest, faltering voice, "that we can all be glad we are in such safe hands under your leadership, President Zo. I have never heard a better, more succinct statement of the mission of this university and law school, and I'm sure my colleagues share my point of view. All of us are grateful to you for stating it so well."

The president soaked up this flattery like a loofah. Mentally, the dean wondered with alarm if the meeting was to become another of Zo's sessions where everyone supposedly reasons together, different points of view clashing in open arena, with the truth emerging at the end in the form of the president's preconceived, personal opinion.

Aaron's unctuous moment in the sun was followed by a few moments of hesitant, stunned silence. The faculty seemed reluctant to proceed.

Then Windy Dave spoke. Windy Dave could have been a close relative of Alonzo Schmidt; his jowly, florid face, topped by a luxuriant mane of white hair, sat atop a tall, large-boned frame that tended, in his later years, toward corpulence. Always attired in a dark suit with an anachronistic watch chain draped between the pockets in his vest, he had risen as if in court to address a jury.

"President Zo, if I may, I'd like to state an opinion which I know is shared by many of my colleagues. I shall be as brief as possible. We all know the law school has problems." The words rolled forth mellifluously. "Serious problems. Nor is there doubt that we possess advantages. We have an excellent location and an able student body. We are connected to a highly regarded university." Zo looked pleased. "Our faculty is talented, our program is diverse, and many students are attracted by the size of the school.

What are we doing, then, to capitalize on these advantages? What are we doing to overcome our weaknesses? The answer is – nothing. Sir, nothing is being done!"

Windy Dave's peroration, his summation to the jury, had begun. Throwing his shoulders back, he locked his thumbs into the pockets of his vest. "And why is nothing being done? It is because – I'm sorry to say – it is because we suffer from a crisis of leadership. President Zo, the ship is foundering." Windy Dave's voice boomed out; unhooking his right thumb, he swung his arm in a wide arc. "Yes, foundering! The cliffs loom from the darkness in a stormy sea. We are awash, taking on green water. And where is our captain? Where is the man who must save us? Where is our solace in the midst of adversity? The bridge is silent. We must man the pumps and lower the boats! Yet we do not have a captain who is taking command. This man, regrettably, is not leading us."

So saying, Windy Dave pointed his finger at the dean. "He is our problem. He is the problem that must be solved."

Although the dean knew the meeting had been called to discuss replacing him, he had not anticipated a frontal, verbal assault. President Zo appeared baffled, as did a few of the professors seated at the table. The dean's face reddened as he wondered whether he should respond. But to say what? His accomplishments were known, although apparently not appreciated. Surely, he thought, President Zo will talk plainly and sternly, as he had said. Now was the time for a strongly worded defense.

The president, however, was mute.

Junker raised his hand and, without acknowledgement, began to speak. "We all admire the dean a great deal. He has always had my strong, personal support," he dissembled convincingly. "The school, however, is at a difficult juncture in its history. We can applaud the past, but the point is not where we've been. It's where we're going."

He stopped. The question of leadership had been raised again, albeit obliquely. With a faint smile, Duxbury glanced approvingly at Junker.

"He's right." Boomer joined the conversation, anxious not to let the moment slip away. "The question is where we're going. I hate to say it, but the question is also the leadership we need to get us there. The faculty needs direction and discipline. We need someone who can pull us together and command the respect of the community."

"I think we should be careful," the Duchess added. "We must proceed carefully to avoid further bad publicity." She stopped speaking and looked around the room, then resumed. "It seems to me the real question we should be asking right now is how we feel about ourselves. If we feel good about ourselves, we can move forward. If we don't, then we're going to be pulled apart as we try to correct things."

And so the discussion continued back and forth across the ornate table, as shadows lengthened within the room. Was the ship indeed in trouble? The crew was unquestionably alarmed, whether realistically or in panic. There was an undercurrent of hysteria. Over and over, the same themes emerged: the need for more applications, more financial aid, more money for new and innovative programs. And lurking behind them all, deep concern about the violence inflicted on a staff member and two members of the student body.

Finally, Junker spoke again. His mustache had been twitching for several minutes. There was an edge, an icy civility to his voice.

"It's not that we can point to any single problem. We can't. But we know the school is in difficulty. And that difficulty is certainly not helped by an unsolved murder in our own basement. I say," Junker began to rap the table, "that something is terribly wrong. Not right. Not right at all. We know what it is. Why beat around the bush? We need better leadership; we need someone who is in charge, who is working with us to solve our problems. We do not need an amiable poltroon. Let's face it forthrightly – we need Edward Elliott to be our new dean."

Throughout this discussion, which had lasted over half an hour, President Zo had been silent. At last he intervened.

"Thank you," he said. "Thank you for this frank and, I must say, very helpful exchange of views. I recognize that many of you are opposed to the dean. Others, it seems, are not or are uncertain. This situation is hardly out of the ordinary in academic institutions. In fact, in any good institution there are always honest differences of opinion. Because it is only through this kind of creative tension that we move forward, it would be appropriate now, I think, to hear from Massoud." He turned in his chair and faced the dean. "Do you have a response to any of the remarks that have been made?"

"Yes, I do," the dean began, his voice low and tentative. Earnestly, he searched the faces before him, and a few faculty members averted their eyes. "Let me say first that I've sat through easier meetings." He laughed nervously. No one joined him. "I appreciate your candor. It can't have been easy for some of you to be so forthright."

He spoke clearly, but he was hesitant, occasionally faltering, as he carefully chose his words. "Naturally, as I'm sure you agree, I see the problem differently. Who can deny that the school is having difficulty or that the police have yet to solve these terrible crimes? But I'm not a detective, and I'm not the problem. When things aren't going well, it's tempting for any group to think that their leader must be to blame. That's human nature. But you have to keep in mind that there isn't any quick fix. It may take several years. So we have to keep plodding forward, one deliberate step at a time."

At the word plodding, Junker glared at him. Boomer raised his hand but let it fall when Zo refused to notice him.

"It's the faculty who set the tone for the school, who make it a rigorously academic place or not. That's an encompassing attitude. It includes teaching and scholarship, and frankly, there's too little scholarship by the faculty and too much outside work…"

Bathroom Bob did not raise his hand to wait for the president to call on him. He simply interrupted.

"How can we write anything if there aren't enough legal pads? Anytime you go to the supply cabinet, it's always half empty."

"What do you mean, it's always half empty?" interjected Fetherheft crossly. "Are you suggesting – and I certainly hope you are not – that we don't do a good enough job keeping you in supplies?"

"No... uh, I'm not." Bathroom Bob looked agitated, and his head jerked to one side. "Well, yes, actually, I guess I am. How are we going to get writing done when there's nothing to write on? I mean, what are we supposed to do, go out and buy our own materials?"

Vice President Caribe looked at Bathroom Bob as if he were demented. "Is there something wrong with that," he half snarled. "Do you have any idea how much supplies cost? I think most of the time that you people steal them anyway."

"No, they do not." Fetherheft spoke again. "We keep those supplies under lock and key. We make sure the faculty won't steal them."

"Who has the key?" inquired Duxbury. Everyone knew the answer, but he feigned disingenuousness.

"Alice Davis, of course – one of your faculty secretaries."

"So," continued Duxbury, "I suppose anyone knowing her well would have easy access to the supplies."

A professor seated across from Duxbury blushed. He was having a well-publicized affair with Alice. He and Duxbury also disagreed frequently.

Quietly, the professor said: "That's a lie, and you know it. I have never helped myself to the supplies."

"No one ever said you did," Duxbury responded sweetly. "How odd that you should think I was referring to you."

The professor's blush deepened.

Fetherheft said bluntly, "I'm not sure what this is all about, but the faculty secretaries report to me – through the dean, of course. There isn't any impropriety in my department. I'm not sure you people recognize how hard we work in the university administration trying to keep you happy." Fetherheft frequently protested her ceaseless toil, partly to cover for the fact that she seldom wheezed to work until mid-morning. She continued: "We do our part. It's about time you did yours. We could see more scholarship and writing out of you people. Indeed, we could. A lot more."

Mattress Head joined the conversation. "It isn't just legal pads," he said. "I mean, okay, everyone knows those are in short supply. It's also pencils. All you keep in supply are #3 pencils, and a lot of us write with a #2. I do, for instance. The mark from a #2 is darker on a page. You can photocopy it more easily. That helps when you're cutting and pasting an article."

"I'd like to add to that," said a faculty member seated next to Fetherheft. "A lot of us use #2 pencils. They're much better when you want to photocopy something that you've written. That's why they're better than using a #3. They're not so light on a page, and when you want to cut and paste, they're easier to work with. Maybe, if we had a more up-to-date copying machine, we wouldn't have this problem."

Fetherheft rounded on the speaker. "Our copy machines," she bellowed, "are state of the art. Let's not blame your lack of productivity on the equipment. That's the carpenter blaming his tools. Come on," she softened, "you can do better than that."

"Okay, okay," said Mattress Head, defensively, "but the pencils are a real problem."

Another faculty member joined the discussion. "I'll second that. And I'd just like to make this point. Several people on the faculty use #2 pencils. You see, a #2 pencil makes a darker line when you're writing. Because of that – and I think this is the real point we're all driving at – it's easier to xerox something you've written when you're trying to rearrange parts of an article. No one wants to rewrite things. It makes more sense to just cut and paste. That's why, for instance, I much prefer a #2 pencil."

Aaron attempted a solution. "Maybe," he suggested tentatively in his nasally voice, "we can find a compromise here. Something that will satisfy both sides. Because I'm sure, even though we haven't heard from them, that some of us prefer a #3 pencil. Why not issue every member of the faculty a mechanical pencil. This could be done when a faculty member gets tenure. Before then, I suppose wooden pencils could be used. Long-term members of the staff could also have mechanical pencils," he added with egalitarian zeal, "and then all we'd need to stock would be different kinds of lead."

"And go to the trouble of buying it," hissed Vice President Caribe, "and having it break, to say nothing of the cost of buying mechanical pencils. Haven't you people ever heard of a budget? And what happens," he sneered, "if someday you come to work and forget your pencil? What then? Do we put you back into wood for the day?"

"The solution, then, is pretty obvious," said Boomer defensively. "What we should do is stock both #2 and #3 pencils. Then the ones who use a #2 can have a darker line on the page when they write. And I think someone said that the advantage to a #2 is that a darker line is easier to photocopy. So the people using a #2 can cut and paste more easily, and, let's just face up to it candidly, those using a #3 won't have that option."

"That still doesn't take care of the problem with the pads," said Bathroom Bob sarcastically. "All the pencils in the world are no good if there's nothing to write on. And, let me remind you all – although it hardly needs saying – we haven't even discussed the problem of erasures and paper clips."

"There is no problem with paper clips," thundered Fetherheft. "How many times do I have to tell you people that we do a good job taking care of supplies."

"Why don't you just look in the file cabinet," responded Bathroom Bob, his head crooked to one side. He was shouting in return. "Just see if I'm telling the truth. Go ahead, take a look. It's filled with fine-line pens and note pads. Nothing else."

"That's not so!"

"Yes, it is!"

"People, people!" President Zo's voice rose above the raucous din. "I mean ladies and gentlemen. I'm sure this is a problem that can be solved. We all want the best for the school." Drumming his fingers on the table before him, he glanced peevishly around the room. "I'm going to appoint a committee to look into our supply situation. I'll ask the dean to be on it, and probably one of the vice presidents, a couple of faculty members, and, I guess", he wrinkled his nose, "a student. We can meet again in a month or so, and by then I assume we'll have a report."

"We don't need a committee," Fetherheft muttered quietly. But it was time to end the meeting. There was a general, relieved sense that a decision about something, anything, had been made. The question of decanal leadership, and the more urgent question regarding the unsolved murders and rape, were unanswered and effectively tabled for the future.

Zo looked about him. No one spoke. Outside, through the ornate windows, the budding trees were muffled in gathering dusk. He concluded, unnecessarily: "This meeting is adjourned."

Chapter Twelve

Some Action Taken

"What was it like?" Mrs. Ackerman asked the question.

It was the day following the meeting.

Head down, the dean had slouched home to his apartment afterwards, where he lived alone. Glumly, he had munched on a dinner of leftover food in his refrigerator, watched television with only desultory interest, and then retired to bed. A weary sleep soon embraced him, but in the middle of the night he woke with a fitful start, restless with tangled thoughts, and lay in the darkness trying to understand what had happened. It was no use. Finally, he switched on the light next to his bed. Propped up on pillows, he distracted himself with reading until the dawn.

Walking into the building the next morning had not been easy. He had not known that he had so many detractors, and he had not been able to finish what he wanted to say at the meeting. Once in his office, he busied himself for a while with minor administrative chores. The telephone rang three or four times, and he responded with false conviviality. The first time it was President Zo, not too subtly congratulating himself on how well he had conducted the meeting. That drew an unseen, arched eyebrow of surprise, but nothing more.

There was left over correspondence to check, which he perused with dispatch, and the teaching schedule for the coming year. The latter was a complicated chart of class hours in each semester, courses taught in each class hour, and teaching assignments for each faculty member. It had been prepared by the assistant dean, and he set about making necessary adjustments. In the midst of this labor, Mrs. Ackerman knocked and immediately entered. She was carrying, as was so often the case, a sheaf of letters and memoranda, which she dumped onto a corner of his desk before sitting down in her usual chair. She looked across at him as he slid the chart to one side. Directly, without introduction or hesitation, she inquired what the meeting had been like. It was a blunt variation of the questions he had asked himself all night. And he was no better able to answer her than he had been able to answer himself the night before.

"I don't know," he said, returning her frank gaze. "I mean, I know what it was like, but I can't figure it out." Placing the pencil nub that he had been twirling between his palms onto the chart, he rose stiffly and walked to the window. There he turned and half seated himself on the narrow sill, his long legs stretched out before him. As usual, he was wearing a tweed herringbone jacket, with patches at the elbows, and a dark blue, silk tie. The tie had a couple of spots on it, a prior misadventure with soup.

Mrs. Ackerman eyed him with an uncharacteristic, puzzled expression. "What do you mean, you can't figure it out?"

"It doesn't make sense. What do they think would change if someone else were dean?"

"Who do you mean by 'they'?"

"Oh… a number of the people who were talking. Windy Dave, for instance. " His remarks still stung. "That clown."

"You aren't going to let someone like him get you down, are you? Everyone knows he likes to make speeches and thump the table. Still," Mrs. Ackerman smiled, "he is likable."

"No, he's not. He's a lying fraud." He spit out the words with vehemence.

"Well," Mrs. Ackerman ventured, "at least you had President Zo to back you up. That must have been a help."

The dean grimaced, then walked to the chair behind his desk and slumped down into it. Elbow on the desk, he cradled the side of his head in his hand. That piece of the puzzle baffled him as much as any other.

"A help? No, I don't think he was any help. With an ally like him, who needs enemies?"

"What do you mean?" Mrs. Ackerman shook her head, genuinely concerned. "You and the president are such friends. He must have taken your side if there was criticism… and it sounds as if there was."

"Plenty of it. Pretty unfair, too, if you ask me."

"What… what did some of them say?"

"I don't want to talk about it… No, I take that back. I do want to talk about it, but I'm not sure I know what to say." He welcomed a confidante with whom he could speak, and Mrs. Ackerman had long since occupied that role. "Maybe it's no more complicated than firing the coach. I mean, if a football team or baseball team isn't doing well, the solution is always to fire the coach. Right?"

"No, wrong. Sometimes it's not his fault. Maybe the players aren't playing well, or there's dissension, and they haven't come together as a team. Sometimes the solution is to trade players."

Mrs. Ackerman was an avid sports fan, following the fortunes of the local teams on television with great interest. She knew the names of all the players, past and present, and their records. Unless one had considerable spare time for listening, it was dangerous to ask her a question on the subject.

"You can't fire these players," the dean said. "They're all tenured. That's part of the problem. We should get rid of tenure, but it will never happen."

Frowning, he stared moodily out the window.

After a few moments of silence, Mrs. Ackerman said, "Anyway, no matter what you say, I'm sure President Zo is on your side. He knows you're doing a good job and that a lot of our difficulties aren't your fault."

"If he knows it," the dean burst out, "why didn't he say it? Honest to God, all he did was sit there like some kind of... some kind of marshmellow... all that garbage about talking tough! And he never said a word when Lieutenant McCallister read the poem."

"Poem? What poem? You never said anything about a poem."

"Yes, of course I... " The dean paused, scratching the side of his head. "You know, maybe I didn't... with all these other things going on. It's weird. It's right here... I have a copy. Zo wrote it out for me." He opened the top right drawer of his desk and, after rummaging for a moment, removed a piece of yellow pad paper.

"Let me read it to you," he said, adjusting his glasses.

> There never were seven,
> But once there were six.
> Five was too many,
> Fours not a good mix.
> Three would be better,
> And better yet two.
> One will be left,
> And she will die too.

"May I see that?" Mrs. Ackerman held out her hand for the paper, then quickly glanced at the writing. "My goodness! It is weird! Have you any idea what it means?"

"None at all... although Allison seems to think it refers to her in the last line."

"Refers to her?" Mrs. Ackerman was studying the poem intently, which was scrawled in the president's nearly illegible hand. " That seems very unlikely. Where was it found?"

"It was taped to the door of Zo's office. A computer printout. No one saw who put it there."

"Perhaps it's a clue." She shuddered. "I wonder who'll be next."

"Next? No, most likely it's just a bad joke."

"I wouldn't rely on that," said Mrs. Ackerman nervously, "unless I knew for sure. Something terrible might happen quite soon."

The dean looked at her across the top of his spectacles. "But surely... well, I suppose it could be... yes, I suppose it could be some kind of warning. Thomas and Kevin could be numbers six and five." Concentrating, he wiped his hand across his lips. "This conversation reminds me that Kevin had spoken with Thomas, and Kevin wanted... rather urgently... now I remember... to talk with the Financial Aid Committee. Of course he never did... how stupid of me not to have thought of that before. I wonder if Thomas – or Kevin – spoke with anyone else."

"How about Ruth Dinsmore?" Mrs. Ackerman volunteered.

"Why her?"

"She was on the committee with Kevin."

"It doesn't seem likely. She'd have said something, I'm sure.

Still... we ought to ask her. In fact, maybe I could get her – in her role as a committee member – to poke around a little bit to see if we can get more information. She knows lots of students... and I suppose it's possible, from her work for the Women's Association and the committee, that she also knows people in the Accounting Office... Yes, that's an excellent idea. We'll ask Ruth to make some inquiries. Maybe she can find out what had gotten Kevin so agitated."

"I'll call her," said Mrs. Ackerman helpfully, "and get her to come in."

"You'd better also contact the new head of the Gay and Lesbian Law Students' Association – whoever that is – and tell him or her that I'll come to their next meeting. I gather they have some ideas about increasing applications. And who knows? Maybe I'll stumble on some leads to what's going on around here."

"You think they'll know something?" Mrs. Ackerman eyed the dean skeptically.

"I don't know, probably not, but I'll grab for a clue wherever I can find it. This place needs a change of attitude, and it would be a big step in that direction to get these crimes solved."

"But that's not your job."

"I think it just became my job," the dean answered. "Lord knows, the cops, as far as I can tell, aren't getting anywhere, and someone has to figure out what that poem means and why our students were killed. And there's something else. It's not just the murders, assuming that's what happened to Thomas, as everyone now seems to be thinking. I never informed the staff that the intruder on the second floor – the one who scared Alice Hodges – might have been a rapist. He certainly terrified Alice, but I concluded there was no assault or attempted rape.

That may have been the right legal conclusion, but I should have warned everyone. The librarian, Henry, urged me to, and he was right. I thought full disclosure would scare away applicants for admission, but look what happened to poor Janet Harbrough." The dean raised his downcast eyes and looked directly at Mrs. Ackerman. "That was partly my fault, and I feel terrible about it. I owe it to people to pitch in and help find the person, or persons, who's committing these awful crimes."

Mrs. Ackerman viewed the dean with an expression of horrified astonishment. "You didn't warn us?" she accused him.

"No, and I've got to make it up to you."

"I suppose you do," she said reprovingly. "But don't make something bad even worse. If the person responsible finds out you're snooping around, you could be in danger, too. I don't think you should do it."

"I don't think I have a choice, and for all we know, I may already be in danger. If the attitude expressed at the meeting yesterday continues, I can't run this place. Someone else will have to be dean."

"You're doing a good job," Mrs. Ackerman said, her tone reassuring yet sober. "You've got to keep remembering that there are lots of people who admire what you're trying to do."

Chapter Thirteen

Another Meeting

The dean went to the meeting of the Gay and Lesbian Law Students' Association about a week later. The meetings of the association were held once a month, sometimes at the school in a lounge or seminar room, sometimes at a private home or apartment. On this occasion the group met in the home of the association's new president, a young woman named Phyllis Hofstadt. Phyllis had close-cropped hair, wore baggy trousers and sported a man's wristwatch. She had been one of the dean's students during her first year, and he liked her. She was bright, genial and articulate.

He drove to the neighborhood where Phyllis lived. It was a nondescript part of town, an area characterized by small, neat, single-family houses interspersed with occasional unkempt dwellings, their lawns unmowed and shades askew. Several pick-up trucks, mostly black, dotted the street and driveways. One had a gun rack.

After parking, the dean walked down the street to the house, feeling conspicuous in his coat and tie and a trifle nervous. He had never been to a gay and lesbian gathering, and he was not sure what to expect. The neighbors, he was certain, would think he was one of them, and he was convinced that all of them – the men anyway – were burly, beer guzzling, tattooed working stiffs who enjoyed bashing gays. It was a salutary lesson to experience the odiousness of discrimination from the recipients' side. He sauntered along, hands in his pockets, trying to appear unconcerned, as if his destination were ten miles away in a different county.

He need not have worried. No one accosted him. The students who greeted him at the door were very friendly and obviously pleased that he had come. There were, perhaps, thirty or so men and women present. Most of them were milling about in the living room and dining room. Cans of beer, two bottles of wine and a plate of cheese and crackers graced one end of the dining room table, and the dean poured himself a glass of wine. Phyllis introduced him to several people standing near the table, most of whom seemed awkward in his presence – a typical reaction; students often want a dean or professor to be present at their functions, but as an ornament and not as another human being with whom to have a casual conversation.

One member of the faculty, an openly acknowledged lesbian, nodded to the dean from across the room. She was the group's faculty advisor and was talking earnestly with a lean, muscular white man of medium height and build. He was facing away from the dean, and he turned to see whom she was greeting. Their surprise was mutual. It was the janitor – or custodian – whose office was directly inside the entrance to the passageway leading to the men's room in the basement. The dean had not hitherto realized he was a homosexual.

But then, the dean knew little about him other than his name, Charlie Traynor. Although Charlie seemed slightly older, he blended into the student crowd and was noteworthy only by his straight black hair, graying slightly at the temples, deep set eyes and even features. After a moment's hesitation, during which his eyes bored into the dean's, he smiled, and the dean did likewise just before Phyllis grasped him by the elbow and led him into the living room.

It was time for the meeting to begin. The students congregated in the room, a few sitting on a sofa or scattered chairs and the remainder sitting cross-legged on the worn carpet or standing by draperies pulled across a bow window at the far end of the room. Phyllis introduced the dean, saying how honored they were to have him as a guest. After his brief response, she asked for a moment of silence in honor of Kevin Pannelli. It was a great loss, she said, to the group and, as many or those present were aware, to Kevin's partner, Charlie, who had agreed to attend the meeting to honor his friend.

Charlie looked around the room, bobbing his head slightly, a wry, awkward smile on his features. Why, the dean thought, the wry smile? He guessed that Charlie had not been informed that he would be present. The dean studied him surreptitiously, but he avoided eye contact. With concealed surprise, he noted that Charlie was wearing New Balance running shoes. The dean was puzzled. Would a homosexual rape an attractive young woman? Surely not, he concluded, and his attention returned to the meeting.

Following her introductory remarks, Phyllis took up the first order of business – whether to amend the name of the club to include bisexuals. Most people, it appeared, had not considered the idea, or thought the change unnecessary, or believed that the change did not go far enough. The dean was reminded of discussions at faculty meetings. The question was tabled for consideration at a subsequent meeting.

Phyllis then turned to the matter that had induced the dean to attend – suggestions for increasing applications to the school. She asked for a general discussion, and many of the students proposed ideas that the dean or the faculty had considered before.

He was forced to remind them that it takes money to make money – or, as he told them, more money for scholarships and a decent library would go a long way toward solving the school's problems.

"Well," Phyllis said after several more comments from the students, "maybe we should turn now to the main agenda item for this meeting." She gestured to a young man seated on the couch. "Gregory, this was your idea. Do you have something to say?"

Gregory stood, then sat down. Nervously addressing his comments to the dean, he said, "We wouldn't have any problem with enrollment if we turned Crabshaw into an all gay and lesbian school. Word would go out coast to coast. They'd flock here."

Everyone seemed to think it was a terrific idea – everyone, that is, but the dean. He could imagine how the Board of Trustees would react, particularly old Harry Stephenson. There would be an uproar from them and many of the alumni, who would reduce or eliminate their financial contributions. Of course, some people on the faculty – Mattress Head, for example, with his florid liberal instincts – would probably be pleased, but everyone else would think that the institution had gone daft.

The students finally got around to asking the dean's opinion.

He said that, putting it frankly, the school would probably lose as many applicants as it would gain. Beating a muffled drum for diversity, he added that of course applications would be welcome from anyone. "But," he asked, "how would they feel if the school limited itself to applications only from older women, or Jews, or white Anglo-Saxon Methodists?" The students picked up that criticism and started arguing among themselves. After a while, the meeting degenerated into private, occasionally heated conversations, and by the time Phyllis accepted a motion to adjourn, the formal proceedings had ended.

His presence at that point being superfluous, the dean decided to leave. Looking around the room, he spotted the faculty advisor and waved goodbye. He noted that she was no longer talking with Charlie Traynor and that Charlie was nowhere to be seen. Phyllis thanked him for coming to the meeting, and he thanked her in return for the opportunity and for allowing him to participate in the discussion.

The dean then headed for the door, but he felt gentle pressure on his elbow as he was leaving the room.

John Vandervoort, a hefty, ebullient student in one of his classes the previous year, asked in his high pitched, earnest voice if he could speak briefly with him. Unlike many students, John did not suffer a lack of self-confidence in the face of an older authority figure.

"Sure," the dean said, indicating a corner of the dining room. "We can talk there."

As they walked toward the corner, the dean said, "That certainly was a touching tribute to Kevin Pannelli. I didn't know he was a member of your organization. You all must have liked him a great deal. It was very nice of Phyllis to mention Charlie Traynor, too."

John squinted and tilted his head to one side. "It was very inappropriate, if you ask me."

"Really? Why?"

"They had a quarrel and parted company a couple of weeks before Kevin died."

"A spat between… well, I didn't know anything about their relationship. Friends? About what – if it's any of my business?"

"It was no spat. They were partners. It was something serious. At one of our parties Charlie screamed at Kevin that he was 'a real scumbag', but the rest of us had no idea what it was all about."

"Interesting… very interesting." They had reached the corner and stood facing each other. "Do the police know about this?"

"I don't know, but I kinda doubt it. They never talked to any of us, but they must have talked to Charlie. He'd be very unlikely, though, to tell them about his personal life and his relationship to Kevin. That's just not the kind of thing we fess up to very readily."

"Yes, I suppose that would be so… " The dean chewed his lip. "Well, I don't suppose that's what you wanted to talk about. What's on your mind?"

"It's probably not all that important, Dean. It's a bit complicated, and I don't feel comfortable bringing it up here. I was wondering if there would be a time when I could speak with you in private. It involves a member of the faculty."

"Why don't you make an appointment and stop by my office. We can talk there. With spring break next week, you may want to put it off for a couple of weeks, but any day is fine… except Thursdays, when the Academic Council has its regular meetings with the president. Sometime in the afternoon would be best."

Chapter Fourteen

Fetherheft

The dean was troubled by John's comments that the inclusion of Charlie Traynor in the tribute to Kevin was inappropriate and that he and Kevin had had a bitter falling out. Perhaps Kevin was killed as a result of a lovers' quarrel, or Charlie might know important details about Kevin's personal life that could provide some explanation for his violent death – or suggest avenues for further inquiry.

He concluded that a call to Lieutenant McCallister or Lieutenant Walsh would be in order. First, however, the dean decided to find out more about Charlie but not speak with him directly. The intensity of his gaze was unnerving, and there was something about him, something ineffable, that said be careful. On the other hand, he imagined that Allison Fetherheft would be a less threatening source of information. As the vice president for administration, who had ultimate responsibility for Building and Grounds, including the maintenance and janitorial staffs, she might know something about Charlie's background. Such information could possibly furnish the dean and the police with leads to more information that might in turn unravel an explanation for Kevin's murder.

Like doing early research for a paper, the dean was messing around, rummaging, trying to ascertain the most fruitful areas of inquiry. He called Fetherheft and asked if he could come to her office to talk with her. As they seldom interacted, except at meetings, she seemed puzzled by his request, so he explained that he wanted to find out more about Charlie Traynor.

"Okay." She spoke slowly, drawing out the word. "Why come to me?"

"Because," the dean said, "he works in a department that reports to you."

"But I don't know him."

"Yeah, but you could find out about him. I'm only asking for a few minutes. The meeting won't take long."

There was a long pause. "You're wasting your time. Like I said, I don't know anything, and this is a busy time of year. We're working on the budget. Anyway, why do you care about him?"

"I'll let you know when we meet."

Again, a pause. Then, finally, with a snort: "Oh, all right. You aren't going to learn anything, and I'm sorry, the meeting will have to be brief. But if you really want to meet, okay, come ahead. How about tomorrow right after lunch?"

The dean agreed, and the next day he rode a city bus across town to the main campus. Fetherheft's office was next to President Zo's, so he had no trouble finding it. A secretary in a reception area did not recognize him, but she responded with alacrity when he told her his name and that he had an appointment. She knocked gently on a partially open door, announced his arrival – he was obviously expected – and ushered him into Allison Fetherheft's office.

The room was not large, but it was comfortably furnished in a modern decor. He noticed the African art immediately. A hanging tapestry, covered with intricate brown and black geometric designs, adorned one wall. Three statues of African women, each carved in dark wood, graced her desk and the top of a low, adjacent bookcase. A couple were performing menial tasks: carrying sticks for firewood and pounding yam in a round bowl. The third, with pendulous breasts and a swollen belly, was standing erect, her back arched backward, looking forlorn.

"Nice art," the dean said without conviction, approaching her desk.

"Thanks." Her expression was opaque.

"You a collector?"

"In a way, in a way." Her expression did not change.

Fetherheft motioned him to a leather chair. Seated behind her desk, she was wearing a pale grey suit with a white, silk blouse buttoned to the neck. Her only adornments were a modest pearl necklace and a gold ring with a diamond setting flanked by sapphires. She stared at him with her small, porcine eyes, her fleshy hands folded in front of her. The uneasy quiet was only disturbed by friendly, student shouts outside on the front walk.

The dean broke the silence. After clearing his throat and wiping his forefinger across his upper lip, he ventured that he wanted to find out more about Charlie Traynor, that he had been informed that he and Kevin Pannelli were homosexual partners and that they had quarreled shortly before Kevin's death.

Fetherheft's expression, hitherto impassive, turned quizzical. "I'm sure you realize," she said, "that we don't inquire into the private lives of our employees."

"Yes... yes, I do. But I thought you might have heard something or that you might share information – information, of course, that you feel it would be appropriate to reveal – from his employment application or evaluation reports."

"As a matter of fact," she said, tilting her head, "I have his application right here." She tapped a file at the side of her desk with a plump finger. "I've gone through it... For goodness sake, stop rattling your foot around inside my wastepaper basket."

"That's not... My foot is not in your basket. I must have been tapping my toe against it."

For a moment, Fetherheft frowned. Then she resumed. "I'm not sure I should reveal this information, although it's a matter of public record. On the other hand, I think you should be warned before you start making inquiries and get yourself into trouble."

"Believe me," the dean said, "I'm not interested in trouble. I'll be discrete, although I do intend to discuss this matter with the police. What's the information?"

"Well... Charlie has a checkered past. We hired him anyway, mainly on the recommendation of his parole officer, and our judgment's been vindicated. He's been a good worker, except for more absences than we'd like."

"His parole officer? What... ?"

"As a juvenile he had a record for petty theft, nothing really serious, but in his early twenties he was sentenced to ten years in prison for manslaughter. It involved a quarrel over money and a fight in a bar, or something like that."

"Heat of passion manslaughter," the dean said, nodding his head.

"Heat of passion? Are we talking about the same thing?"

"Yeah. Heat of passion, voluntary manslaughter, they're the same. It means an intentional killing while in a violent rage or other extreme emotion. It's a way for the law to reduce a murder to manslaughter when there are mitigating circumstances."

"Thanks for the lesson. I didn't know that. Anyway, I hope

you get my point. Let the police do the snooping. A lovers' quarrel could have led to a homicide, particularly if Kevin was cheating on him. It's happened before. But for your own sake, I wouldn't get involved in it."

"It's not as if I want to." The dean looked at her as evenly as he could. For the first time, he noticed a cloying scent of perfume. "But you know the law school's in trouble. Unless we get our applications up, we'll be hemorrhaging money. And no one wants to apply to a school with a member of our staff raped on school grounds and a recent, unsolved murder in the basement, and maybe another murder off school grounds. You yourself said that I should find out what happened. We've got to discover who committed these crimes and get him behind bars."

"And you think that you – you personally – are the one to do it? That wasn't what I had in mind." Her tone was sarcastic, and as she spoke, one of her eyebrows rose slightly.

"Yes... well, actually, no. I mean, I'm not qualified, but I want to help. I've even asked Ruth Dinsmore – you know Ruth, I'm sure – to try to find out what was bothering Kevin Pannelli and, I guess, Thomas Headly."

"Find out what?" Her eyes narrowed.

"Find out anything she can. Talk to students." The dean faltered momentarily. "I forgot to ask you. Even talk with you and people in the Accounting Office. Find out what was bothering them – maybe, I'm not sure – about financial aid or whatever. Just get some information I might pass on to the police."

"You should have spoken with me first if you're thinking of asking Miss Dinsmore to poke around over here." Fetherheft shifted slightly in her chair. "We'll cooperate, to the extent we can, but we've got a great deal of work to do. And most of our files contain confidential information and are not open to students."

"But they were open to Thomas."

"That was obviously different. He was a student employee. Frankly, I can't see what you're driving at. There's nothing wrong, and Thomas wasn't upset about anything. I don't know where you got that ridiculous idea... And stop tapping my wastepaper basket with your foot."

The dean looked down, then up. Fetherheft was glaring at him. "I just want to ask around, that's all. Just ask around."

Chapter Fifteen

The First Letter

"This is our first real break," said Lieutenant McCallister. He was seated in the dean's office, again in a dark suit, lounging back on the couch by the coffee table. The dean was seated opposite him in an adjacent chair, leaning forward with his elbows on his knees.

"We searched the janitor's office very thoroughly the day of Kevin's murder, and we didn't find anything of interest – no weapon, no incriminating correspondence, nothing. We also talked with him at length after the sexual assault." Lieutenant McCallister spoke slowly and deliberately. "If you can loan us the key, we'd like to go through his office again. We may need a search warrant for any private compartments in his desk, and we're certainly going to need one for his residence. We'll go there soon."

"Be careful," the dean said. "As I told you, he has a conviction for a violent crime."

"Don't worry. We can take care of ourselves. Where's he now?"

"Usually on the second or third floor at this time of the day, but he could be almost anywhere."

"We'll find him. Walsh will be here any minute. He'll be coming down to the station with us to answer questions."

"I'll sure be relieved if he's the guy who did it," said the dean. "Then maybe we can get this place back to normal – well, as normal as it ever gets."

"Your theory's not a bad one." Lieutenant McCallister said. "A violent quarrel over infidelity, sure. Another manslaughter and very possibly a first degree murder. All possible. Now what about Kevin?" he continued. "We need to find out more about his life outside the school. Damn, we never thought of interviewing the members of your – excuse me, what did you call it – some kind of gay and lesbo club. Dean, we'd like to have their names and where we can reach them. We'll start with the president, Phyllis What's Her Name, and your former student, John – the one who tipped you off. I'd like to know, too, whatever else he wanted to talk with you about."

"No problem, no problem," the dean said. "I'll give you the names and their current addresses. And maybe they can give you the names of other students who knew Kevin well. Or Thomas, for that matter."

"I think, Dean," Lieutenant McAllister said, "that if either student belonged to other organizations, we should get the names of their officers, too."

The lieutenant rose to leave, shaking the dean's hand. 'This has been very helpful, and we'd like to talk with you more about those missing financial aid funds. We'll get back to you soon. There may be some connection we don't see at this point. Keep that student working on it."

"If you need me," the dean said, "I'll be here – or I'll leave word where I can be reached for the rest of the day." He walked Lieutenant McCallister to the door. "On your way out, you can pick up that key from Mrs. Ackerman and, if you don't mind, tell her to come in. I'd appreciate it."

The dean retreated to his desk as Mrs. Ackerman entered the office and placed a small stack of letters and memoranda on the corner. She stood before him, her careworn hands resting on the back of the chair in which she usually sat. Her floral print dress, a size too small, pulled in small wrinkles at her waist.

"Well, I hope that was a successful meeting," she said, fishing for a clue as to the content of the conversation. The dean nodded his head but said nothing. Mrs. Ackerman tried a different tack. "The meeting with Ms. Fetherheft didn't go well, I gather. Was she rude?"

"I'll say she was rude. Never even bothered to get up or say goodbye. She went back to work, reading a report, and it took me a couple of minutes before I realized that I'd been dismissed. She's like a bull in a... no, like a cow – a big, surly cow."

Making a clucking sound, Mrs. Ackerman slowly swung her head from side to side. "That wasn't nice of her. Not nice at all."

"No, it wasn't. Maybe, though, at the end of our meeting, it was partly my fault, although the mistake was innocent enough."

"The mistake...?"

The dean exhaled. "Oh, all I did was comment on a photograph on her bookcase. It was of a beautiful, thin woman, and I asked if it was her daughter. She stared at me, and her mouth fixed into a thin line. Then she said it was a photo of her, when she was younger. When she said it, her voice sounded almost metallic."

Mrs. Ackerman shook her head again. "Some people eat when they're unhappy. Like my Walter. He eats too much, although in his case I think he just likes food – and his beer. He'd have to like food, because Lord knows my cooking isn't that good. My mother told me I'd never hang onto a man if the way to his heart was through his stomach." Mrs. Ackerman laughed heartily. "My mother said that... " Her voice trailed away, as she saw the dean sitting quietly, tapping his fingers on the desk. Lamely, she concluded: "Was she any help at all?"

"No. She didn't want me trying to find out anything about the janitor. She knew some things about his past... I can't tell you about them. She warned me that he might get violent if I started asking questions. And she wasn't friendly or cooperative when I said Ruth might speak with her."

"I think she's right." Mrs. Ackerman leaned toward the dean. "You shouldn't be getting involved. You don't know what will happen, and it's not your responsibility."

"I've already told you," the dean said, his voice rising in exasperation, "that it's become my responsibility. I'm not turning back, and I'm not calling Ruth off. We need information."

"You're being stubborn. You always get this way." Mrs. Ackerman turned to leave the room. "Anyway, speaking of Ruth Dinsmore, there's a letter in that pile that will interest you. Unless I'm mistaken, it's from Ruth's father. Maybe it will convince you that she's not your best choice."

The dean riffled through the items on the corner of his desk and found the opened envelope. In Mrs. Ackerman's job description, it had never been clear whether she was supposed merely to open his mail or read it as well, except envelopes clearly marked personal or confidential. From the start, she had chosen to read the mail and, moreover, comment on it. The dean even caught her once, when she thought no one was looking, holding a personal and confidential letter to the light, hoping to catch a word here and there through the envelope; that particular envelope was pink with feminine handwriting on it, and she sniffed it also for any tell-tale odor of perfume.

It was Mrs. Ackerman's oft-stated position that you can never be sure about men. Sometimes the nicest ones are the worst. But she never detected perfume.

"I think Ruth's father is being unreasonable," she volunteered, having paused at the door.

"Yeah, I'll say." With furrowed brow, the dean was already reading the letter. "Let me finish it." He perused it again. The letter read as follows:

Dear Dean Ansari:

A couple of weeks ago when I walked through your school for the first time with my daughter, who is a graduating student, I thought I was on foreign soil. And I don't mean Switzerland or Denmark. I mean very foreign soil. Being in the export-import business, I know what I'm talking about.

Let's start with the dirt. It being springtime, it's possible that boots and shoes get muddy. There's no excuse, however, for not sweeping it up or for dingy corridors, cracked tile and linoleum floors, peeling paint and poorly illuminated stairwells. Are you just used to it that way, back wherever it is you came from?

Telling the janitors to clean up the place would be a good way to start. That kind of directive must come from the top. Of course, we don't call them janitors anymore. Since FDR, under the Democrats, we call them custodians or custodial engineers or some such crap like that. The title isn't important. Put the boys with the brooms, mops and pails to work, and if they won't do the job, fire them and give the assignment to the faculty.

No one would know the difference. My daughter pointed out one of your professors talking with a group of students. He's the one with the big mop of bushy hair who, I gather, is called Mattress Head. No wonder. I couldn't tell who was the most slovenly, him or the students. I'm not one of you academic types, but I suggest a dress code. You'll never get coats and ties back on the teachers and students. We've come too far for that. But just requiring people to have clean clothes would be a step in the right direction.

Another thing. You keep that man away from my daughter. I don't like the look of him. We come from good stock. The Dinsmores can trace their heritage back to Puritan New England through my paternal grandmother.

Your library is a disgrace. This may be an overstatement, but half the shelves don't seem to have books. Not that anyone was in there studying. Moreover, I'm surprised there's no cafeteria and no gymnasium. Where do the students go when they want a bite to eat, and what do they do when they need to exercise? They all look like four-eyed, scrawny eggheads who could use a workout on bar bells. Perhaps you could employ them in the winter to shovel snow, or form them into work crews to give the school a fresh coat of paint.

This has not been an easy letter to write. As you may be able to tell, I'm upset. Legal education isn't cheap. My daughter is a loyal student, and she tells me and her mother that she's getting a good education. I hope so. However, if I may be straightforward, perhaps blunt, it is difficult not to conclude that the place is being run by an incompetent. Well meaning, no doubt, but an incompetent nevertheless.

Please inform me of the steps you are taking to remedy the deficiencies I have brought to your attention.

Looking forward to your response, I am
Very truly yours,
Frank Dinsmore

PS. My daughter also showed me the main university campus, and while we were there, standing on the sidewalk, she introduced me to a vice president who was walking by. Or waddling by, I wasn't sure. It was a memorable vision. Her name is Dusterhead or Fetherheft – something like that – and Ruth said that at one time her nickname was Dean Dreadnaught. If it wouldn't be tactless, you should direct her to a strenuous exercise program. Half of her would still be too much.

"Oh for Christ sake!" Nettled, the dean threw the letter down on his desk. "Do you have any other goodies in there?" He pointed to the pile of letters and memoranda that Mrs. Ackerman had brought in and deposited on the corner of his desk.

With a worried frown, she shook her head in the negative. "No, that's the only one. I thought you might want to answer it right away. That's why I brought it to your attention."

"You're right." He blew air at the ceiling. "We shouldn't sit on it." The dean swung his chair in a semicircle toward the cabinet beside his desk and picked up a microphone. "I'll dictate a response right away."

Dear Mr. Dinsmore:

Your recent letter arrived today, and I thought it would be best to respond without delay. Over the years I have enjoyed hearing from the parents of our students. Their constructive criticism and helpful comments have often been very useful.

Your letter, however, did not fit in that category.

I am sorry to disappoint you, but I am as American as you, albeit a naturalized American, and America is the "wherever I came from" and where I was educated, if Dartmouth and Yale Law School qualify.

Let me address your comments about the school.

Crabshaw is not a wealthy institution. We receive some indirect support from the university, but for the most part we rely on income from tuition. It would be enormously helpful to have a large endowment, but like most law schools, we do not have one.

Our tuition is already high but insufficient to cover all our costs. As a result, we do not have the most modern facility, but fresh paint is not a guarantor of academic excellence. Moreover, most law schools do not have cafeterias. They are not eating and drinking establishments. Neither do they have their own gymnasiums (or should I say gymnasia?). Athletic facilities are available to Crabshaw students at minor inconvenience on the main university campus.

To borrow from your language, your remarks were well meaning, no doubt, but were stated in a way that was unhelpful. If you visit us again, I invite you to come to my office so that I can answer any questions and clear up any misconceptions you might have.

> *Please don't hesitate to get back in touch with me if you have any further – and useful – observations about the school.*
>
> *Very truly yours,*
> *Massoud Ansari*
> *Dean*

Mrs. Ackerman had been listening while he dictated. "Are you sure you want to send that?" she queried.

"Yes. I should have made it even tougher, but that's not my style."

"All right," she said. "I'll get the letter prepared for your signature.

Chapter Sixteen

The Plotters Meet Again

"Pssst! Over here!"

"Where?"

"Behind the stack."

"Oh, right." Boomer walked around the stack of books to a table at which Junker and Duxbury were seated. He was wearing white pants to celebrate the advent of spring, white shoes, and a dark red shirt that flared before his bulging neck. "Aren't you afraid people will see us here?"

"Who? Our colleagues? In the library? Not a chance." Duxbury murmured the response.

"So why the secrecy? How come you wanted to meet in the library? Why don't we just meet in one of our offices?"

"Remember last time when Aaron came and stood at the door," said Junker in a low tone of voice. "He's an ingratiating blabbermouth. We don't want that to happen again." One side of his mustache twitched.

"Okay," Boomer said, slowly comprehending. "Where's Duchess… uh, sorry, Jane? Is she joining us?"

"Yes." Duxbury spoke, again in a sibilant murmur. "She had to go to a meeting, but she should be here soon."

"What do you want to talk about?"

"We need to assess the meeting. It wasn't a complete success, and it seems to me we need to think through what more needs to be done."

Boomer looked first at Duxbury, then at Junker. "I thought it was pretty good," he said. "What did you expect? We certainly got a lot of points across and a lot of things said that haven't been said before, particularly in front of Zo."

"True," hissed Junker, "but nothing was resolved. There was no vote of censure, no condemnation. Just when I thought we might be getting somewhere, the dean got to speak, and then that idiot Bob had to start carping about pencils, for Christ's sake. Or was it paper?"

"Fetherheft was in good form."

"She's a loud-mouthed pain in the ass."

"I see," said Duxbury softly, addressing Junker, "that you're more waspish than usual today. Our friend here makes a good point. Maybe we got out of the meeting all we could expect. After all, what did we think was going to happen? Maybe we should think of it as a good opening move in a campaign."

Junker was about to reply when they heard a soft tread in an adjoining aisle. The group fell silent.

The intruder, obviously female from the sound of her footfalls, hesitated, then moved forward. She stopped, either to browse, select a book, or listen. In a few moments the cautious tread continued down the aisle and around the corner.

It was The Duchess, attired in brown slacks and a near matching beige sweater over a white blouse. She would have fit comfortably into any informal, country club get-together or a casual lunch with friends at the local garden club.

"Well!" she said, her voice resonating in the muted silence of the room, "I was afraid I might not find you."

"Shhhh," interjected Junker quickly. "Not so loud."

"You don't need to worry," The Duchess answered with a

look of furtive apprehension. "I didn't see anyone." Her voice fell to a whisper. "Why are we here?"

Duxbury glanced down modestly at his interlaced fingers. "We were just talking about that when you arrived. The question is whether the meeting went as far as we could have reasonably hoped, or whether it should have gone farther, perhaps to a motion for a vote of censure."

"Vote of censure?" Her hushed tone was shocked.

The three men looked at The Duchess. Realizing that a further reaction from her was expected, she said, after a thoughtful pause, "Well, I guess I didn't think it would go that far… It seems to me that we got as much as we could expect. We don't want to cause trouble or have a lot of hurt feelings… This has got to be done carefully."

"You can't make an omelet without breaking eggs," responded Junker in a harsh, grating tone.

Duxbury eyed him carefully. "I suppose so. Of course. But you can cook it in a hot pan for two minutes, and have it taste like leather, or you can cook it slowly and produce a masterpiece. I'd prefer a masterpiece."

Having delivered this comment, he leaned back, at the same time adjusting his eyeglasses, and, in a nervous mannerism, he stroked the nether tip of his goatee. He was, as usual, dressed in an old, rumpled suit. Junker, in contrast, was dressed impeccably. His white shirt lacked a high, stiff collar, but his fastidious correctness made up in every other respect for the omission. Today, moreover, his close-shaven hair accentuated the bullet like quality of his skull, and the points on his flaring mustache seemed to have a particular elan.

The group sat quietly for a few moments. The Duchess was the first to break the spell.

"A masterpiece? I'm not sure I like to think of it that way... What we're doing, I mean. This is not a work of art we're trying to create."

Junker interrupted. "I don't care how it's done, as long as it's done. This school needs discipline. It needs blood and iron."

"The real question," said Boomer, "is what more needs to be done? Where do we go from here?"

"Yes... that is the question," Duxbury murmured. "Where do we go from here? Does anybody have any good ideas?"

"How about another meeting?" ventured The Duchess. With a plump hand, she reached for a lipstick and small mirror in her purse and casually inspected her makeup.

"No, too soon," responded Duxbury. "We need an incident or a fresh issue to discuss. Otherwise, it will look like we're just calling meetings to rehash old stuff and complain."

"Well, how about a petition signed by the faculty, or as many of them as we can get?"

"No, too soon for that, too."

"Why?"

"Why? Because... " Duxbury cleared his throat. "Look, we've only been complaining about the dean's leadership for three or four weeks, at least publicly, and not everyone agrees with us. He isn't going to turn things around, believe me, but we're going to seem unfair if we don't give him a chance to respond."

Boomer offered another suggestion in a noisy whisper, "You know, Zo and the dean are friends, or used to be. After what you told us, I wasn't surprised Zo didn't defend him more at the meeting, but then Zo isn't president for nothing. He knows how to protect his own ass." Boomer barked a short laugh, betraying the clandestine site of the meeting.

"Quiet, you dolt," whispered Junker, "and get to the point!"

Boomer ignored the insult. "What I'm trying to say is that we've got to get to Zo from another direction, from above. Which is to say, from the Board of Trustees. Zo might listen if it's a Board member talking to him. He reports in that direction, not to us."

Duxbury looked appreciatively at Boomer. "Interesting. Very interesting,"

"The problem is," The Duchess interjected, "that no Board members are likely to speak with Zo as if the ideas are their own. They'll say they were speaking with members of the faculty. With us. And then Zo will know where the ideas came from. He sets our salaries, you know. I think we should be very cautious about going down that road."

A damp blanket having been thrown on the idea, Duxbury nibbled at his lower lip and again tugged at his goatee. He was reflecting. He took out a wrinkled handkerchief and began polishing his glasses. "For now I guess we'll have to be patient. Let's see what turns up. Something will, you can bet on it. I suggest we meet soon after graduation. By then we'll know what to do."

"Will you set the date and time?" The Duchess asked.

"Yes."

"OK, that's settled," said Boomer. "I move we adjourn."

"Not so fast. Hold on a minute."

"Why? It's time to go."

"We all want to go," said Duxbury, "but it will look strange if four members of the faculty are seen leaving the library at the same time."

"It will look strange," broke in Junker, "if one member of the faculty is seen leaving the library."

Smiling slightly, Duxbury agreed. "We need to spread out the times of our departure," he said. "Let's see. I suggest we leave in fifteen minute intervals. Why don't you go first." He nodded at Junker. "Then Jane. I'll go last."

That left Boomer in third place with a half hour enforced delay. He folded his hands in silent resignation and stared glumly at the bookcase in front of him.

Charlie

Chapter Seventeen

Reconnaissance

Charlie Traynor was interrogated at length in the police station, but he refused to admit to the homicides or the rape. He was released as a person of interest, not on the hook but not off it either. Lieutenant McCallister informed Dean Ansari that Charlie would be returning to work. "We're keeping an eye on him," he said.

In the early afternoon two days after receiving this information, the dean, clearly frustrated, told Mrs. Ackerman that he was going down to the basement and have a look around. "If Charlie Traynor's not in his office," he said, "I'm going to take a peek. There's something fishy about that guy, and I just want to make sure that the police didn't miss something."

"Oh my God." Mrs. Ackerman looked at him in dismay. "Haven't the police already been there? She had been drinking coffee, and she placed the coffee cup deliberately beside her computer. "Now don't you go to the basement and start looking around. That's just asking for trouble. I can feel it. Promise me you're not going to do such a foolish thing."

"No." He drew out the word. "I'll not promise any such thing. I'm just going to walk around. Don't get yourself in a tizzy about it."

Mrs. Ackerman drew in the corners of her mouth and shook her head while her eyes scrutinized the dean. "I'm sounding like a cracked record," she mumbled to no one in particular. "There's no use repeating myself." Seated at her desk and now staring fixedly at her computer screen, she did not look up as he walked through the office, a certain sign that she was preoccupied, annoyed, disapproving or some combination of all three.

The dean strode down the corridor and descended the stairs at the far end. As he passed the metal door with the crash bar that opened to the parking lot, he recalled, for a flickering instant, snow sprayed across the floor and the thrumming squeal of tires outside.

The hallway in the basement, flanked by student lockers, was well lit from overhead lights in round, frosted globes hanging from the ceiling. It was late afternoon, and no one was present. Unmuffled by the sounds of thronging students, the dean's footsteps thudded on the linoleum floor. He turned into the short, dingy corridor at the end leading to the men's room and the furnace room beyond.

On his immediate right the door to the custodian's office – to Charlie Traynor's office – was closed. Instead of stopping, he entered the men's room across the hall and looked around carefully. Overhead, fluorescent lights illuminated the room. Two booths were to his right, in one of which he had discovered the female shoes and the seated Raggedy Andy doll. Next to the booths, farther on, three urinals occupied the remainder of the right wall.

A counter with three sinks ran the length of the end wall, a ceiling-high mirror above them. The left wall, painted white, was blank. For a moment, seeing a patch of mismatched paint, he concluded that someone must have written graffiti on it. Then he remembered Kevin Pannelli's bloody handprint sagging to the floor. The dean had found Kevin slumped before the booth next to the urinals; he could have been attacked there, the dean thought, or he could have staggered there after receiving his mortal blow somewhere near the door.

He stood in the room and studied the location where the body had been found, trying to reenact the scene in his mind. Someone had obviously bludgeoned Kevin to death. Was he killed outside the restroom or inside? As best he could recall, no trail of blood led there. If Kevin stumbled on a crime as it was being committed, why weren't there signs of a struggle? And why the weird doll and the shoes? It didn't make sense.

The dean scratched his head and saw his frowning reflection in the mirror. No wonder the police are having difficulty. To add to his confusion, it seemed inconceivable that two reputable law students could be killed within two days of each other unless, unknown to school authorities, they were involved in something like dealing drugs and were slain in a drug deal gone sour.

If Charlie Traynor had been in his office when the killing occurred – and not outside or in another part of the building mopping the floor, replacing a light bulb or some other menial chore – he might have heard something: voices, a snatch of conversation, a shout of alarm. Of course, the dean thought, the police must have spoken with him about these possibilities, but it wouldn't hurt to ask his own questions. Where had he been? What had gone wrong between him and Kevin? The police hitherto may not have known anything about his relationship with Kevin, and the dean knew from practicing law that sometimes you don't ask a question because you don't know enough to realize that you should.

Anyway, wasn't he one of Charlie's superiors, if not in the

direct chain of command? Certainly he could speak with him. That was easy to say to himself, but his palms were moist and his hand trembled slightly as he knocked on the janitor's office door. There was no response. He knocked again. Gingerly, he turned the knob, flicked on the light switch just inside and walked in. The cramped cubbyhole of a room seemed even smaller because of the mounds of clutter scattered across the floor and on a battered metal desk in the center just inside the door. Cans of paint and cleaning fluid, tools, light bulbs and manuals of one sort or another were jammed into shelves on a bookcase behind the desk. After stepping tentatively inside, he partially closed the door and saw a calendar tacked on its back. Featured on it was a handsome, muscular young man, nude from the waist up, standing by an automobile. He also noticed that the date of Kevin's murder had been circled by a felt tip pen in red ink.

The desk appeared to serve more as a repository for maintenance supplies than as a workstation. Hardly any of its surface was visible. Columns of toilet paper occupied at least half of it; plastic containers of cleaning fluid, paint remover, disinfectant and detergent were stacked on another third; and a large monkey wrench lay carelessly on the corner of the desk nearest the door on top of a magazine about hunting.

Picking his way around a stepladder propped against a side wall, the dean circled the desk and, as quietly as possible, opened the top drawer of a bank of drawers on the right side. The drawer was filled to the top with papers, and, upon carefully removing them, he discovered a metal box that had been closed by a simple clasp. Reaching down, he removed it and, after creating a space on the desk by pushing back some plastic bottles of cleaning fluid, placed it on the edge of the desk. Then he opened the clasp and lifted the lid. Inside was an envelope with the name Charlie scrawled across the front.

Reaching into the box, he picked up the envelope and saw that it wasn't sealed. Fumbling with trepidation, he opened it and withdrew a sheet of paper on which, in a neat, inked hand, was a letter to Charlie. It was a mere paragraph in length.

The letter began with a bland statement, common enough to lovers, that the writer had not seen Charlie and missed him. He glanced down and saw that it was signed *"with deep affection"* by Kevin Pannelli. The text related a tearful, urgent apology, beseeching forgiveness. What followed next made the dean breathe in deeply and stiffen his torso and neck. Kevin stated that he had been unfaithful and was HIV positive, that he had known for many months, and that he had not wanted to tell Charlie because he was afraid that this news would end their partnership. *"I'm so sorry,"* the letter ended. *"I know I should have told you, and now you may have it too. I pray fervently and constantly that you do not."*

The dean had risen from his crouching posture and was standing, letter in hand, when a black silhouette blotted the entrance to the room.

"What the fuck are you doing here?" a voice snarled. The figure at the door was Charlie Traynor. "And what the hell do you think you're doing going through my desk?"

The dean looked down at the letter in his hand, then up, his neck hunched between his shoulders, and he dropped the letter haphazardly into the open box before him. "I was... I was... " No further words emerged. He stared at Charlie, mouth agape, not knowing where or how to move.

"I'll tell you what you were doing, you miserable piece of shit," Charlie growled through clenched teeth, his voice low and menacing. He took a step forward and grasped the handle of the monkey wrench that was lying on the desk. "You were reading my mail. Weren't you? Weren't you?" His voice rose as he spoke.

"I was just... I mean, I have a right..." The sentence trailed off into silence. The dean's eyes were fixed on the wrench that Charlie had raised in his clenched hand to the height of his chest. Why, the dean thought, was I so engrossed in examining the contents of the box that I failed to hear footsteps in the corridor?

"I've killed a man for as much," Charlie said, his dark eyes, like burnt holes, holding the dean immobile. "And you ratted me out to the police. I'm not going to prison again, if I have to kill you and everyone else in this place."

The dean found his voice, although it was hoarse and trembling. "I had every right to tell them you were Kevin's partner."

"And make them think I did it."

"Well, did you? You had good reason to be angry, if that letter means anything." The dean gestured downward at the box on the desk. "Did the police see this?"

"No, I had it hidden and just put it there this morning. And now I suppose you'll tell them – more reason for them to come after me."

"Let me ask again. Did you kill Kevin, or do you know who did?"

"The answer is no to both questions, and the cops already know that. For Christ's sake, I loved Kevin. And now the police will be on my ass again, thanks to you, you bastard." Charlie took a step forward, still brandishing the monkey wrench.

In a moment of desperation, the dean said, "Did you kill him with that?" He raised his arm to ward off a blow.

"You put that down this instant." It was Mrs. Ackerman standing at the door. Her tone was sharp and laced with reproof. "Charlie Traynor, I'm ashamed of you."

Charlie pivoted about slowly and gaped at her. He lowered the wrench until it hung opposite his thigh. But he didn't relinquish it. With what seemed like infinite care, his lips clenched in a tight line, he scrutinized the cause of interruption, his dark brows furrowed together. It was as if the dean, Mrs. Ackerman and Charlie were frozen in some ghastly tableau.

Then a male student shouted to another student in the corridor, and they heard the sharp clang of a locker door striking an adjacent locker. The second student replied, "Aw shit, I thought that asshole'd never let us out. Jesus!" Another locker door banged open. The speakers were standing around the corner, and they were obviously unaware of a potential murder only a few feet away.

Mrs. Ackerman took advantage of the opportunity. The dean had never realized that she could show such presence of mind. "Dean Ansari," she said, "I think you should come with me," The student voices subsided. The dean walked around the desk and, tucking in his stomach, slid behind Charlie to the door. As he did so, Mrs. Ackerman took a step backward, then wheeled to join him. Glancing behind him, the dean saw Charlie still standing, wrench in hand, gazing after him and Mrs. Ackerman, his face a mask of malevolence.

Obviously embarrassed, the student who had spoken busied himself in his locker without turning around. The other student, a lopsided smile on his features., greeted the dean cordially as he and Mrs. Ackerman walked hurriedly past him,

As they reached the far end preparatory to ascending the stairs, other students had started into the corridor.

Sensing a commotion behind him, the dean turned. A dark figure, arms gesticulating wildly, had burst from the small passageway that he and Mrs. Ackerman had just left. One of the two students was staring at him, rooted before his locker, while the other scuttled away with a jacket in his hand.

"God damn you, Dean Ansari," Charlie shouted. "God damn you to hell."

Chapter Eighteen

Charlie

Puffing from exertion, Dean Ansari and Mrs. Ackerman mounted the stairs rapidly. As they neared the third floor, Mrs. Ackerman glanced nervously down the stairwell and saw – or thought she saw – Charlie Traynor entering the stairwell from the basement corridor.

They both heard the sound of someone with heavy work boots laboriously mounting the stairs, taking them two at a time. She nudged the dean, then pulled at his elbow. "I think he's coming after us. Hurry!"

When they reached the third floor landing, the dean hissed, "Run!" as they quickened their pace down the corridor toward his office suite at the opposite end. The dean was agile and speedy, but a sprint for Mrs. Ackerman resembled a fast waddle. Nevertheless, they entered the door to the outer office just as they saw Charlie emerging, panting, from the stairs. He still had the wrench in his hand.

Past a startled receptionist, the dean and Mrs. Ackerman sped across the outer room and into the dean's office. The dean slammed the door and locked it. Retreating to his desk, he picked up a heavy paperweight and stood, irresolutely, with his newly acquired weapon in his hand.

"Quick," he said to Mrs. Ackerman. "Call the police and tell them to get here – to my office – as soon as they can."

Mrs. Ackerman reached for the telephone and a rolodex

file of numbers on the desk. Riffling rapidly through the file, she found the name of Antwan McCallister and punched in the number.

At that moment the dean heard the receptionist cry out as, having risen to determine what was happening, she was rudely shoved out of the way. There was a brief commotion followed by a rattling of the door knob, then a harsh banging on the door.

"Let me in," Charlie shouted. "Let me in, God damn it." The blows on the door grew stronger, and the dean wondered if it would hold. Neither he nor Mrs. Ackerman shouted back. She huddled next to him as she mutely handed him the telephone.

"Hello, hello, is this the police?" he said with urgency.

"Yes," answered a familiar voice. "What is this? Who am I speaking to?"

"Lieutenant McCallister, it's Massoud Ansari at the law school. Please send help here as soon as you can. Send it to my office. Charlie Traynor is banging on the door, and I think he wants to kill me."

"Hang on, Dean. I'll get a patrol car there right away, and I'll come myself. You say you're in your office?"

"Yes. Hurry!"

"Coming right away." There was an audible click as Lieutenant McCallister slammed the telephone down into its cradle.

As these last words were spoken, Charlie shouted through the door: "I'll wait out here if it takes all afternoon. I want to talk to you." He ceased banging on the door.

"You can talk to the police," the dean shouted back after wiping moisture from his upper lip. "I just called them, and they'll be here any minute."

"What'd you do that for?" Charlie's voice still sounded grating and angry. "Jesus, you're an asshole."

Mrs. Ackerman had been standing by the dean's desk, but she tottered over to the sofa and plumped down. "Are we safe?" she inquired in a low voice. "That man is a maniac."

"I think so," the dean responded, also in a low voice. "The door is holding. That was a brave thing you did, coming downstairs and rescuing me. I don't know what would have happened if you hadn't been there."

"It was very foolish of you to go there," she said, "and I told you so. I just had a feeling something might go terribly wrong. And it..." She turned her worried, frazzled face to the window. Outside, in the distance, she could hear the rising wail of a police siren as the car drew closer to the school. Then it stopped, followed by a car door slamming shut and the sound of running feet.

Charlie Traynor heard it too. He banged once more on the door with his fist. "I didn't do it, Dean Ansari. You've got to believe me. I loved Kevin, and I would never have killed him."

For an agonizing two minutes, there was silence, then a polite knock on the door. "Who is it?" the dean rasped. "The police," came the answer. Cautiously, the dean opened the door. Two patrolmen were standing there. The receptionist was standing near her desk, wordlessly clutching her throat. Otherwise, the room was empty.

The dean was standing just inside the door to his office, still holding the paperweight. He stepped tentatively forward and looked around the outer office. "Where is he? Where's the man who was here?" Indicating ignorance, the receptionist shook her head dumbly.

"Charlie Traynor, the janitor, was here banging on my door

with a monkey wrench in his hand. I think he wanted to kill me… and now he's gone. You'd better check downstairs for him," the dean said, still panting slightly. "Try the basement first, where the lockers are and the janitor's office. It's down a short passageway at the end. He may have gone back there. Or he may be hiding in the interior staircase, just outside the door. Try there, too."

Shortly after the two patrolmen departed, Lieutenant McCallister entered the office followed by two additional police officers. "You all right, Dean?"

"Yeah. I think so. Just a bit shook up. I've no idea where he went."

Mrs. Ackerman stepped forward and spoke directly to Lieutenant McCallister. "That Charlie Traynor is a very bad man. He was going to hurt Dean Ansari with that wrench he was holding in his hand. You've got to catch him."

"We'll do our best, ma'am." The lieutenant conferred briefly with the officers who had entered with him, and they left to search the building.

"Please sit down," the dean said. "Maybe Mrs. Ackerman can get you a cup of coffee."

"Good idea on both counts. I need to find out what's happened here."

As he had before, Lieutenant McCallister sat on the couch. The dean again sat in an adjacent chair. Mrs. Ackerman retreated into an adjoining, small closet near her desk and returned with a steaming cup of coffee.

"So what's this all about? What happened?"

The dean related the entire incident, and near the end Lieutenant McCallister began to wag his finger. "You warned Joe and me to be careful, Dean. I guess you didn't take your own advice. You should leave snooping around to the police."

"I know. Or now I know. It was pretty dumb."

"Have you any idea where Charlie could have gone?"

"No. Not at all. But what do you think about that letter to him from Kevin? There's plenty of motive for you, if you need it."

"Yeah, but nothing more than we already guessed. It doesn't provide any corroborating evidence that Charlie committed the crime. And it doesn't say a thing about Thomas Headly."

"Oh," the dean said, deflated. "Well, what do you make of the fact that he denied doing it. More than once. Those were some of his last words before he took off."

"Not much. Criminals usually deny they did it. It takes a long time, sometimes, to get a confession. Maybe he's telling the truth, maybe not. He's entitled to plead not guilty. These psychos – and maybe he's one – can be awfully adept at conning people."

After a brief silence, the dean brightened slightly. "One more thing... I saw a hunting magazine on his desk. Janet Harbrough was raped by a man wielding a hunting knife."

A resigned expression on his features, Lieutenant McCallister replied, "There are lots of hunters in this town. That's weak circumstantial evidence. It's suggestive, but awfully weak."

"So we're no closer than we were before."

"I'm afraid so. Except now we have certain proof that Charlie has a violent temper – a temper bad enough to hurt people. You'd better be careful. And he fled, which suggests guilt, although it doesn't prove it. He could have run away for other reasons. He's probably aware that he committed an assault and maybe false imprisonment. And you said he's really scared of going back to prison."

The two men sat in silence. Lieutenant McCallister sipped his coffee and then, after placing the drained cup on the coffee table, stood up. "Thanks, Dean," he said. "And don't ever hesitate to call. We've got a bad situation here, and we still don't know if more bad things will happen."

"No, I should thank you, Antwan," said the dean, also standing. "I can call you Antwan, can't I? And call me Massoud."

Near the End of a Difficult School Year

Chapter Nineteen

Ruth Reports

"Then I went to Charlie Traynor's office," the dean said, stumbling slightly over his words, "and he wasn't there. I noticed he had a calendar on the back of the door with the date of Kevin's murder circled in red, and then I started to go through the top drawer of his desk."

It was a week after their encounter with Charlie, and he was speaking with Mrs. Ackerman in his office. She eyed him quizzically. "And that's when he came in?"

"Yeah, and he got really angry, and I'm so glad you followed me."

"So am I."

"Where is he now?" the dean continued. "You say he hasn't showed up for work all week?"

"It seems so. No one's seen him. I got a maintenance man to check his office, and it doesn't look as if anything's been touched. Except that calendar... the one you mentioned on the back of the door... that's gone. I asked the man if he'd seen it – you couldn't miss it – and he said no, there was no calendar."

"How about that box where I found the letter?"

"I don't know. If you want, I'll call Lieutenant McCallister and see if he'll look for it. Anyway, the police probably have it already."

"I shouldn't have gone down there."

Mrs. Ackerman exhaled slightly, and her features softened.

She looked as if she was repressing a smile. "You're the dean of the law school. You have a perfect right to be in the basement if you choose, and it's none of his business why you're there." She spoke emphatically. "But I was concerned, you know. I didn't like the idea of you rummaging around in his office, and I'm so glad nothing happened."

"Something almost did." The dean paused and glanced at a note that Mrs. Ackerman was holding in her hand. "What've you got there? Something for me?"

"Yes, it's from Ruth Dinsmore. She'd like to see you around 9:15 this morning."

"That's just about now. When she arrives, show her in."

Mrs. Ackerman went to her desk, and moments later the dean heard her murmur a greeting outside the door. Almost immediately thereafter, Ruth knocked gently and entered.

Once again, the dean was taken by surprise. He still had not erased the image from his mind of a Ruth Dinsmore who looked like a junior bag lady. But this Ruth Dinsmore – the new, refurbished version – was actually attractive, attired in tan slacks, a faded coral, cashmere sweater, flats and with her hair falling loosely to her shoulders.

"Hi," she said, shaking her head slightly so that her hair curled against her neck. "May I sit down?"

"Oh. Sure, sure. Of course." Having risen from a seated posture, he sat down again abruptly so that his chair jolted backward a couple of inches. Ruth eyed him with a broad smile. It was hard for him to know whether she was being friendly or was amused. She eased herself into the chair usually occupied by Mrs. Ackerman and crossed her legs at the ankle.

The dean cleared his throat and tried to sound

authoritative. "So, what's up? Is Prigley behaving himself? I hope that's not what brings you here."

"No, it's not," she again tossed her head slightly. "We're actually getting along rather well. To my surprise."

"That's good. I can't say I never had doubts." There was an awkward moment of silence. "So then, what's the problem?"

"I thought," she said, "that you might want to hear from me about how my, ah, research is going. It seemed to me it was time to make some kind of interim report."

There was another awkward moment of silence while the dean frowned, trying to recall what research she had been doing. Then he remembered. "You know," he said, "I've been preoccupied. I should have asked you to come in long before now. My fault, absolutely my fault, and my apologies." He had been examining his fingernails and looked up at her. "Have you found out anything?"

Ruth exhaled and returned his glance with a slight frown and a penetrating stare. "Yes, I have, and no, I haven't. It's very strange."

So what else is new, the dean thought to himself. "In what way?"

"I went to see Ms. Fetherheft to ask if I could speak to people in the Accounting Office who knew Thomas or Kevin and to see what they'd been working on. I thought she would be pleased that someone would be making these inquiries. I mean, we're all in this together, aren't we? But she wasn't pleased. Not at all. She started yelling at me and told me to get out. It was very unprofessional, and I should have told her so, but I was so surprised that I didn't know what to say. All the people in the office could hear her. I just got up and walked out. I was kind of shaken. And then a couple of days later I got a phone call from a young woman in the office who I know, but not terribly well. I've worked with her in the past on the accounts for the Women's Association. She wanted to talk with me, but she seemed nervous and asked if we could meet after work at O'Doul's – you know the place – where all the students hang out. She said that way it wouldn't be obvious that we were meeting, because we might both be there anyway. Well, I met her. I mean, for God's sake, I felt like I was in some kind of spy movie, like I should be jumping in and out of subway cars to avoid being followed. She was sitting in a back booth, facing away from the door. And the awful part is that I didn't learn that much from her, although I sure got the feeling that something fishy is happening. Like, really not good. She said that Thomas had been working on the law school's financial aid files, and she – that is, the woman I was talking to – caught him one afternoon making copies of them at the xerox machine. I gather the staff isn't supposed to do that without permission, and Thomas asked her to be quiet about it. She liked Thomas, and she didn't say anything. A few days later, she heard Thomas arguing in Ms. Fetherheft's office. Nobody ever does that, she said. It was low and angry sounding. When Thomas walked out, she said he looked pretty shaken."

"Did she hear what they were arguing about?"

"She didn't say. I don't think so. I gather Ms. Fetherheft did make him turn over the xerox copies, but I think he kept some. A couple of days later Thomas came back, argued loudly with Ms. Fetherheft, cleared out his desk and took some papers with him. And that was the last she saw him. The next day, he was dead."

"Holy sh…" The dean checked himself. "Do you think there was some kind of connection?"

"I've no idea. None. The woman I spoke with did say that she checked secretly a few days later, and the financial aid files were gone. She didn't know where. Maybe into Ms. Fetherheft's office, but there was no way she could check that out."

"That makes no sense. We've got complete copies of the files here."

"Maybe. Or maybe you don't. Or maybe someone figured you'd never look at them very carefully."

"Oh." The dean was speechless. It was strange all right, and he couldn't make any more sense of it than Ruth. He stared blankly at her, then, a bit embarrassed, shifted his glance to a corner of the room.

"You've done a good job," he said finally, nodding his head in affirmation. "But where do we go from here? It doesn't seem you can get any information from the Accounting Office." He knitted his brow. "What's with Fetherheft anyway? Why does she have to be so damn possessive and uncooperative?"

"Perhaps," Ruth ventured, "I could talk to students who knew Thomas and Kevin. I've no idea who they are, but I'm sure I can find out. They might know something or at least a hint of something."

"Good thinking. Yes, keep checking and keep me informed. And, you know, it might not be a bad idea to stay in touch with that woman in the Accounting Office. Maybe she can be our – what's the word? – mole? She seems to want to cooperate. She should keep her eyes open… but I'd let the dust settle for a few days."

Ruth rose to depart, and the dean joined her. Looking at her with frank admiration, he started to walk around his desk in order to see her to the door. His thigh hit a corner, and with a loud "oof," he performed an involuntary, unceremonious bow.

Awkwardly, he righted himself, his face reddening, and blurted, "Well, I guess that's it… ah, goodbye… yes , , , and good luck."

"I'll be back in touch soon," Ruth said, suppressing a smile. Her gaze was level and deliberately solemn.. When she reached the door, she turned. "Oh, by the way, I almost forgot. When I was home last weekend, my father gave me a letter to give to you. I told him he should send his own letters and not make me a messenger, but you know…" She sighed. "Anyway, here it is."

Returning, she handed the letter over, then quickly walked out of the room. Yes, I do know, the dean thought to himself. Squelching the urge to put off until tomorrow what he could do at the very moment, he slit the envelope open and started to read.

Chapter Twenty

The Second Letter

Dear Dean Ansari:

Thank you for answering my last letter so quickly. I had not expected such promptness, but then you probably have more time for letter writing than those of us who have to meet a payroll.

Not only was I surprised by the speed of your answer, I was also surprised – and, frankly, pleased – by your candor. I like people who stand up for themselves. That's the American spirit, and I now understand you are probably as American as the rest of us, even if your parents were undoubtedly immigrants. You show more spunk than most of the spineless liberals who have taken over our institutions of higher education, and even though you may not have a backbone yourself, I detect signs of gristle. That's good.

I have another reason to thank you. That daughter of mine, who is one of your third year students, seems to have a beau, and I gather you are partly responsible. To be honest, I never thought it would happen. I met the young man, and he seems pleasant enough, although he could use a few tips on how to dress in polite company. Ruth will take care of that.

My daughter is a determined person, like her father. In all modesty, she gets many of her fine qualities from me. For a while, when she was growing up, I worried that she might turn out to be like her mother. I long ago suspected that my wife operates in a total vacuum, particularly at the tedious parties we attend.

But why trouble you about my personal life? On a more germane subject, you write that Crabshaw needs money. Who doesn't? If you liberals had any sense, you might try earning it, but instead you and your crowd just tax the productive sector of the economy, so there isn't enough left over for charity, and then piss the money away on welfare and other fluffy social programs.

Nevertheless, I agree that you've got a real problem, if the looks of your school are any guide. Perhaps I can be of help. Ruth will soon be one of your graduates, and I want her to be proud of her alma mater. No one feels good about saying they went to a dump, and to be frank (no pun intended), that's what you have.

I doubt you will get much help from your alumni. The Crabbies – yes, I've heard their rather accurate nickname – aren't likely to come up with the kind of jack you need. And, if you'll forgive me saying so, I doubt any foundation will support you. Why would they fund a law school? The last thing we need is more lawyers; it would be like donating money to breed locusts.

We've got to find another source. You are absolutely correct that the school needs an endowment. In fact, it needs an endowment large enough to produce income that will eliminate any operating deficit, provide scholarship funds to attract able students, and furnish something extra for special projects. An attractive student lounge or even, if I may say so, a nice cafeteria should not be out of the question.

This gets me to the main purpose of my letter. I can't be of much assistance right now – although perhaps I can be in the future – but I can help raise your tuition income a small amount. To be specific, I would like to recommend a student for admission. He is the son of a man with whom I do a great deal of business in Africa, and I have encouraged him to apply and further his legal education in the United States. The mail from his part of the world is sometimes slow, but he has already sent you a completed application form that I secured from Ruth, and it should arrive very soon.

The young man is talented, and there is no question in my mind that he will be an able student, probably one of your best. I recommend him to you with confidence and enthusiasm. We don't need more lawyers, but, as the saying goes, there is always room for a good one.

Of equal importance, this applicant comes from a very wealthy family. By this I don't mean enough money to purchase a summer home and a fancy car. I mean oil wells, vast land holdings, an international trading company and enough money in secret Swiss bank accounts to buy and sell Illinois. As an alumnus, he is destined to be influential in his country, and you'll never have to ask anyone else for alumni giving. He will put Crabshaw on the map.

In this day and age, the Africans are getting to be real people. You will not make a mistake by taking prompt action in this case.

Very truly yours,
Frank Dinsmore

P.S. Regrettably, I shall be away on business at the time

of Ruth's graduation and therefore will not have the opportunity to meet you. My wife will attend to represent the family.

Chapter Twenty-One

The Outing

Although it was nearly midday, there was a light on in the office of the Women's Association. Inside, seated next to each other at a battered metal table, Ruth and Prigley were almost at the end of a job that had consumed the better part of the morning. Only once had there been an interruption. Ruth had left for about a half hour to go to the dean's office to ensure that funds were available for the mailing that was occupying Prigley's time. She had chatted merrily with Mrs. Ackerman while the latter retrieved a budget document from a file cabinet and ascertained that an allocation to the Women's Association for mailing expenses had indeed been made. When she returned, Ruth edited minutes of the last meeting and finished drafting letters to participants in a forthcoming conference sponsored by the association. Prigley was stuffing envelopes.

Glancing at the diminished pile in front of him, Ruth said, "It looks like there are only three more to go."

"Yes," he replied absentmindedly, "there is – just a few."

"Prigley?"

"What?"

"There *are* a few." The words were uttered in a firm but good-natured manner.

Prigley laughed at the correction. He put down an envelope he was holding and looked at her. He was smiling. But there was a directness in his expression that did not escape her. Ruth averted her eyes, returning her gaze to the letters on the table.

As she did so, her hair parted at the neck and fell in graceful waves across her shoulders. For no reason she could discern, she had stopped wearing it in a tight bun. And there was now a hint of makeup: a slight darkening above her eyes that accentuated their luster, and a pale trace of lipstick. Her clothes, also, while plain, suggested slender elegance.

A greater transformation, however, had occurred in Prigley. He still wore jeans, but now his shirt was tucked in. More astonishing, the shirt was clean and had a button-down collar. It had been purchased on a rush order through a catalog filled with pictures of clothing for affluent, self-conscious yuppies. And wonder of wonders, his old, scruffy loafers were gone, replaced by a pair of topsiders which still had their recently purchased, store odor.

"Are you free for lunch?" he asked.

"I guess so."

"If you're busy, we can walk around the corner and just grab a sandwich. That would be fine with me."

"All right. " Ruth still seemed reluctant, as if she were at war within herself. Then her hesitation crumbled. "In fact, my first exam isn't for nearly a week. There's no reason to hurry. I wasn't planning to start studying until tomorrow."

A broad smile creased Prigley's face. "If that's the case, why walk around the corner? Let's grab a couple of sandwiches and something to drink and drive out to the reservoir. It's really nice, now the leaves are mostly out. We can have a picnic."

"A picnic!" It was Ruth's turn to smile, and her eyes flashed eager expectation. "Why, I don't think I've been on a picnic for two – no, no, not since I was in college." She touched Prigley's arm. "That would be wonderful. Finish those envelopes while I make a phone call, and let's go."

Ruth picked up the telephone and, holding it to her ear, casually punched a number into its base on the desk. After a moment, she spoke informally to a woman at the other end, informing her that she and Prigley were "going to the reservoir for a picnic" and that she would "not return until mid-afternoon." In an uncharacteristic, pleading voice, she asked whether her "meeting with the provost could be delayed until later in the day." An objection was voiced, to which Ruth responded: "It's just a brief meeting to make sure we have final approval to spend extra money on our conference. Really, it's just a formality. It can wait until tomorrow. Please tell Ms. Fetherheft that I'll be there at any convenient time, but not in the next couple of hours. And please do stop by the office after you're done there and look over the address list."

"Who was that?" Prigley asked after Ruth put down the telephone, a trace of defensive suspicion in his voice. Standing, he placed the last envelope onto a stack in a box on the table.

"Oh… Barbara," Ruth answered vaguely, picking up a beige sweater that had been thrown across a chair. "You've met her. She works part-time in the provost's office. She's also very involved in the Women's Association, but usually she's not here when you are. I expect she'll be over in a few minutes, but we'll miss her."

Ruth threw the sweater over her shoulders and looped the arms across her chest.

"Why did you have to tell her we're going to the reservoir, as if we have to report in?" Prigley asked, frowning.

* * * * *

On the same day, the dean was seated at his desk staring vapidly out the window. He had just finished returning phone calls; no meetings demanded his presence; and Mrs. Ackerman had removed a batch of memos and letters, each signed or initialed in his neat hand, to be dispatched to their various recipients. Sunlight slanted brightly through the streaked windowpanes. Idly, he tried to recall when they had last been washed, but he could not. It occurred to him to ask Charlie Traynor to attend to it, although technically Charlie could ignore his request, as he reported not to the dean but through the university's Department of Building and Grounds to the vice president for administration.

Charlie Traynor. His mind played with his image. Could Charlie be a piece in the puzzle, and might the answer to that question have been in the box in his desk drawer? After toying with the idea, he abandoned the effort. Tilting his head back, the dean surveyed the world outside. The trees were laced with ripening leaves, a few late-bloomers betraying a film of green where the baby fingers of leaves had emerged. Daffodils and jonquils were bunched in beds along the walks in sprays of yellow and white.

It was two weeks since he had received Frank Dinsmore's second letter. Mrs. Ackerman re-entered the dean's office, another sheaf of letters and memoranda tucked under her arm. The dean was sprawled in his chair, daydreaming, the chair tilted back and one foot propped on his desk. There was a visible hole in the sole of his shoe.

"I figured it out," she said, dropping the stack, as always, onto the front corner of his desk.

"Figured what out?" he replied languidly, not curious about Mrs. Ackerman's observations about life – indeed, anxious to forestall any conversation.

"The poem."

"Oh?" He removed his foot from the desk, glancing up as he did so. "Why... what do you think it means?"

"It means the Financial Aid Committee. I've been thinking about it ever since you told me. There's no other good explanation."

"Mrs. Ackerman," he said slowly, in a tone of gentle exasperation, "you haven't done your math. There are three professors and a student on the committee – that makes four. The poem starts by referring to six people who will be killed."

"You're forgetting that Kevin was a member."

"That makes five. Please! You have to add another person to make it come out right." He was irritated by what he regarded as an imbecilic interruption. "Allison Fetherheft thinks it refers to the employees in the Accounting Office, and that the 'she' at the end will be her."

"But," Mrs. Ackerman continued gamely, albeit flustered, "I'm really referring to the people who have – or had – some responsibility for financial aid. That would have included Thomas Headly."

"Yes? And the 'she' in the last line?" His question was delivered with acerbity.

"I'm guessing it will be Ruth Dinsmore. I don't know why, but I'm guessing that the student members... and that would include Thomas... will go first. I've thought... well, it just seems to me that Thomas must have known something, and he must have told Kevin because it had something to do with financial aid, and now Ruth is fishing around, and whoever did this terrible thing must be after anyone who knows something about financial aid. Eventually, that would be all the members of the committee."

"My God!" The dean sat, stunned, staring at the Bierenstok painting on the wall of his office. "Or maybe it means me instead of Thomas. That would bring it to six. It's another possibility."

"I suppose so," Mrs. Ackerman said with a worried shake of her head. "But I still think Ruth is the 'she' in the last line and will be next."

"Where is Ruth? We've got to warn her."

"She was in here about an hour ago," Mrs. Ackerman replied. "She was heading back to the Women's Association office to do some work." Mrs. Ackerman looked distressed. "With Prigley, I think."

Quickly, the dean reached for his telephone, dialed dexterously and rapidly, and spoke with a person at the other end. Was Ruth there? No? Did the person "know where she was going and when she had left? Yes, yes, you've been very helpful... Is this Barbara? Yes, this is Dean Ansari. Please tell Ruth that I'm looking for her if she comes back."

"Where is she?" Mrs. Ackerman asked.

"She left about forty-five minutes ago with Prigley for a picnic at the reservoir. I'm going out there and find them. You stay here in case she returns and calls."

"Be careful," Mrs. Ackerman beseeched him. "Please do be careful."

* * * * *

His task with the envelopes completed, Prigley stood up to leave. Ruth turned out the light and shut the door after them. Talking animatedly, they walked side by side down the steps of the building and along a path leading to the street. The delicatessen, where they were headed, was almost within view.

"I'll order a couple of tuna fish sandwiches," Prigley said, "and a bag of potato chips. Would you like to get one of those small bottles of wine and some plastic glasses?"

"I don't… " Pausing, she shrugged. "Oh, why not?… Do you like tuna fish sandwiches?"

"Yes. Very much. I guess that's why I suggested them."

"So do I." Ruth touched Prigleys's arm again. "Where's your car? You surely weren't thinking we'd go in mine. It's too far away."

"No, I thought we'd go in mine. It's only a block from here, in front of the place where I live."

They completed the purchase of their supplies and walked, side by side, to a car that was very much like the old Prigley. It had not yet been subjected to Ruth's discerning eye. Clean when it left the factory several years before, it had seen only rainwater since and never a flake of soap. Rust from too many harsh winters was spreading along the bottom of the fenders and doors. Inside, Prigley removed papers and an old rag from the front passenger seat so that Ruth could sit down, but she had to place her feet delicately on the floor near a half-filled, plastic container of oil. Carelessly, Prigley threw the bag filled with lunch and the bottle of wine onto a backseat covered by a beach towel and by-gone class notes and text books.

With a few complaining coughs and sputters, the car started. The reservoir was out of town, nearly ten miles away. The journey commenced along a city avenue lined with shops and stores, but quickly they came to an area of large, older houses. Most were of wood, with comfortable front or side porches, and trees newly decked with leaves dotted the broad lawns and spread over the adjacent sidewalks and streets.

That pleasant scene gave way to new developments, barren on former pastures and hillsides stripped of foliage. The residents had begun planting to return their haunts to forest, but they would be gray, and their children gone, before shade would protect them in the summer heat. Until then, the houses did not look so much planted as thrown indifferently on the ground in a spasm of tasteless avarice.

After ten or fifteen minutes, talking about their courses and professors, Ruth and Prigley started to drive through rolling, open countryside. Ruth spied Holstein cattle at the end of a dirt road in an enclosure near a barn with a sagging, corrugated tin roof. To Prigley she explained with delight that the scene did not seem real; it reminded her of a pasture depicted on a postcard or in a nineteenth century painting hung for sale in some cluttered antique shop.

And then, finally, they came to a sign on the right that said RESERVOIR. HUNTING AND FISHING STRICTLY FORBIDDEN. VIOLATORS WILL BE PROSECUTED. Just beyond the sign a dirt road led to a small parking lot and, farther on by way of a leafy path, to a rustic landing where canoes could be rented. With a pang of uneasy misgiving, which surprised her, Ruth noted that only three cars were parked there. They would have the lake, with its large, surrounding tract of wooded land, almost entirely to themselves.

Prigley, however, was exuberantly cheerful. After parking, he reached behind him for the lunch and bottle of wine, then stepped outside, opened the trunk, and removed a blanket. It was a beautiful day, warm but not humid and without the clouds of insects that would arrive in summer.

"Let's go! The trail leads this way," he said, pointing the way to an opening in a split rail fence on the opposite side of the parking lot from the path to the boat landing.

He started off. Ruth ran to catch up with him.

"You didn't forget anything?" she inquired.

"No, except maybe you for a moment."

He laughed and reached over to take her hand. Ruth felt a faint shock go through her, as if she would draw it back, but she did not.

"Where are we going?"

"There's a beautiful cove – and, if I remember right, a grassy bank – up this trail and then off to the right about half a mile. I thought we'd go there."

"Okay."

"So, now, finish telling me what you were saying."

"You mean about Mattress Head?"

"Yeah."

"There's not much more to say. You know, he's awfully bright, but he doesn't know how to control the class. I just got bored, so I raised my hand and started arguing with him. I thought he'd see it was a joke, but he never did. He's so righteous and humorless."

Prigley said, "That's the part that got around school."

"I guess it did." Ruth giggled and looked up at him. He responded with a smile and swung their interlocked hands up in the air. Ruth skipped to keep pace with him.

They had crossed a field and, by a fallen tree, entered a wood that covered a low hill. Ferns lined the path, and around them were firs, white pine, oak and birch trees. The last stood like clumps of white sentinels amidst the green. By a large, moss-covered boulder, Prigley took the trail to the right. It led across a ridge and through a dense, brush covered hollow to the edge of a small clearing that sloped down to a cove.

"Careful!" he said. "Make sure you don't step in poison ivy."

But there was none. Walking in silence, they traversed the clearing to a large pine standing at the farther edge near the water.

"What about here?"

"It looks perfect."

Prigley spread the blanket on a patch of grass. Dropping the bag of lunch, he kneeled and busied himself opening the bottle of wine. Ruth sat down next to him and looked around.

The spot they had chosen was indeed perfect. The clearing, a flower strewn meadow, was ringed with trees. So was the cove that, from their perspective, seemed more like a pond. It emptied into the larger lake behind a spit of land covered with rock and pine that jutted into the water a scant fifty yards in front of them. Reeds and rushes hugged the shore, and a flock of ducks paddled noisily in the distance.

Ruth peeled a peach and placed the cut pieces on a napkin. Prigley handed her a plastic cup of wine and removed the wrappings from the sandwiches. Seated next to each other, looking out toward the water dancing in the sunlight, they slowly consumed the picnic lunch. The day was warm, and Ruth removed the sweater that she had flung earlier across her shoulders. A few ants found some crumbs on the blanket. Prigley brushed one of them off his arm and reclined back, squinting into the sun, his head cocked to one side as if listening, while Ruth remained seated upright.

Now, he thought, now is the time to do it. He could feel his palms growing moist. There'll never be a better time.

"It's a beautiful day, isn't it," he said.

"Oh Prigley," Ruth looked down at him, "you couldn't have picked a more beautiful place. I'm so glad we did this."

She folded her arms around her upright knees, resting her head on her forearm. In so doing, her hair cascaded down over her lower legs, and to Prigley she never seemed more beautiful.

But despite her apparent poise, Ruth also was caught in the fluttering potential of the moment. She believed they were alone. What's going to happen, she mused. To the question there was no answer, only a slight constriction in her breathing, a catching, imperceptible to anyone but herself.

"I wish some of those ducks would swim over here," Prigley said. "We could feed them our leftovers." Propped on one arm, he reached over with the other and touched the back of her neck.

But Ruth struggled to her feet and walked to the bank. "Here ducks," she cooed, "here ducks. We have some food for you." The ducks, however, were much too engrossed in their own important affairs, and they ignored her.

With a shrug and a smile, Ruth returned to the blanket.

And still Prigley hesitated, caught on the tremulous lip between action and inaction, courage and fear of being rebuffed. He started to say something again about the ducks, then changed the subject.

"When I was a boy, visiting relatives in New England, someone told me – maybe my Uncle – that I could write home on birch bark. Have you ever done that?"

"No, I can't imagine how it's done."

"Well, first you find a birch tree." He smiled and Ruth giggled. "Of course. We passed some in the woods walking over here, which is what reminded me. And then you cut a thin layer of bark – just the outer, white part – off the tree. Except that's probably not good for the tree. Usually there's bark lying around on the ground, pieces of it, 'cause the tree just seems to shed it. Or you peel off a bit the tree's just about to get rid of anyway.

I'm not talking about a big piece. When I was a boy, I wasn't talking about long letters either. You know: 'Dear Mom and Dad, I'm fine. Hope you are. Love, Prigley.'" Ruth giggled again. "The stuff you write on is just like, maybe, thick parchment or something like that. It shows you've been in the woods."

He stopped talking. Ruth did not respond. She was sitting, her arms around her pulled-up knees, looking out at the water. The sunlight dappled her hair. From behind the promontory, its silhouette dark as the pines from which it seemed to emerge, a canoe paddled by a solitary passenger slid gracefully into the opening that separated the cove from the rest of the lake.

"Would you like to see what I'm talking about?" Prigley asked.

"What's that?"

"The birch bark."

"Sure. " But her voice sounded reluctant.

Prigley sat up abruptly next to her, oblivious to the intruder into their solitude drifting closer in the canoe. Ruth's eyes, now less than a foot away, were level with his own. He swallowed involuntarily.

"Ruth?"

"Yes?"

"May I kiss you?"

He leaned forward. For a moment she held back, but the poorly constructed dam gave way, an edifice in disintegration. Ruth inclined her body toward his, surrendering to a long, lingering kiss. They separated, looking wonderingly at each other, smiles flickering below dancing eyes, and kissed again.

"Ruth," he blurted, "I'm in… I'm in love…"

"Hush, Prigley… don't say it!"

"May I touch you, too?"

"Oh, Prigley! You're not supposed to ask! And there's someone…"

Still staring steadily, intently, into her eyes, he had placed one arm around her waist and with the other, now around her shoulder, had pulled her close beside him. Obliquely, Ruth saw that the figure in the canoe had risen to a standing position with what appeared to be a stick pointed at them. The bullet struck the ground where, only a moment before, she had been partially reclining.

The recoil from the rifle caused the figure in the canoe to lose balance, and the rifle, now aimed too high, propelled a second bullet through the branches above them. It ricocheted among the leaves. Then, as if in slow motion, the flailing figure toppled backward into the water as the canoe capsized. The rifle, flung into the air, disappeared into the lake with a small splash. A pair of ducks rose from the cove, furiously beating their wings, as the sound of gunfire reverberated from the surrounding rocks and hills.

For several seconds, neither Ruth nor Prigley could comprehend what had happened. But Ruth had seen a pinprick flash from the muzzle and the figure's wind-milling fall, and she quickly understood the gravity of their situation. Grabbing Prigley's shirt, she struggled to her feet, pulling him with her.

"Run! Run!" she cried. "We must get to the protection of the trees."

The figure from the canoe was now splashing clumsily in shallows near a rock on the shore of the cove. Its clothing hung heavily from a pair of massive arms. Otherwise, the cove was still. The crackle of rifle fire had died away. A breeze softly bent the tips of the grass by the water, and the circling, dark green trees stood silently, gently stirring, under the vault of blue sky.

* * * * *

The dean had been often to the reservoir. It was a frequent destination for runners and hikers on its interlaced trails, and renting canoes was a popular option for families and lovers. The boat landing was controlled by the Parks Department, an arm of the city government, and, once buds had appeared on the trees, its employees usually removed the canoes from winter storage on racks in an elongated, adjoining shed.

Nevertheless, traffic on the water was usually scant until the summer months when warmth and vacations brought young people and families flocking to the lake.

Partly for that reason, the dean guessed that Prigley and Ruth had rented a canoe. A boating accident in water still cold from snow-fed streams would be a fitting crime, hard to detect. He drove, therefore, to the parking lot nearest to the landing, and as he was turning to enter, a departing car accelerated toward him. He jammed his foot on the brake pedal, and his car shuddered to a swerving halt as the other car roared past him with a clearance of two or three feet. The entire episode lasted only seconds, far too short a time for him to note important detail. He did glimpse the other driver, albeit poorly – an individual with a floppy hat (or was it wildly disordered hair, he could not tell), dark sunglasses and an arm encased in a drenched sleeve thrown up across the wearer's face as if to avoid detection. The figure seemed large in sodden, bulky clothing. Once the car had sped by him, it accelerated again and, screeching around a curve, was quickly lost to sight.

His car having stalled from the sudden stop, the dean restarted it and entered the parking lot, where he parked near a sign on the split-rail fence marking the path to the landing. Highly unnerved, he left his vehicle to lean on the fence for several minutes to regain his composure. Why had the other car been fleeing the parking lot? Who had been chasing the driver? Was it safe to go on to the landing? What if Ruth had taken a trail instead? And how could he know that she and Prigley had parked here and not in some other location? He reflected with mounting anxiety that a murderer was loose and he was unarmed, yet he had a life to save, if possible.

These thoughts were never resolved, because, just as he was about to walk cautiously to the boat landing, he heard a loud crackling in bushes on the other side of the lot. Trembling, he crouched behind his car. Prigley emerged into the opening, followed immediately by Ruth. Looking fearfully about, they were running toward a car.

The dean stood up. "Prigley! Ruth! What's going on here?"

"Oh my God," Ruth cried, "it's the dean." She shielded herself behind Prigley, who stood irresolutely, facing Dean Ansari.

"I'm here to help you," the dean shouted. "What's going on? What's happening?"

"Here to help?"

"Yes, damn it, here to help! What's going on?"

"Someone was out... was out on the lake." Ruth stammered, "trying to shoot at us... trying to kill us. We've got to get out of here."

"I think that person has gone," the dean said in the most

reassuring voice he could muster. "Whoever it was left here in a big hurry just as I arrived. Get in your car and follow me. We're going to the police."

Chapter Twenty-Two

The Third Letter

Lieutenants McCallister and Walsh pursued every lead. Even the dean was questioned, albeit briefly, as he was able to verify his whereabouts without difficulty. One of the detectives drove to the boat landing and spoke with the Parks Department employee who had been on duty at the time of the shooting. This pimply youth, his usual ennui rattled by the hint of unwanted trouble, spoke volubly, if unhelpfully, about the afternoon's events.

Boat rentals were infrequent on weekdays at the beginning of the season, so he had no trouble remembering the person who had rented the canoe. It was at this juncture, however, that his unhelpfulness began. He recalled a heavy, squat individual swathed in military fatigues and wearing a slouch hat over what might have been a blond wig or might have been an inordinate swatch of frowzy hair. The person wore sunglasses – natural enough on a bright day – and as best he could recall did not have any indication of a beard. But the voice, either affected or real, was raspy in a masculine way, and while the posterior suggested femininity, the gait – again, either affected or real – appeared masculine. The individual was carrying a long package but responded negatively when asked if it was fishing gear.

He had thought, in a vague way, that the new dispensation for tolerance was shaking all the nuts out of the can, and he was fascinated by this obvious specimen. But he made no effort to expand upon his limited responsibilities and dutifully took the rental fee after asking the person to write down a name and address in a worn ledger in case of loss or breakage. The handwriting, in large, block letters, defied subsequent analysis; it indicated that the individual was a Peter Marinovich who lived at 139 Spruce Street. Naturally, no person with this name could be located and, indeed, there was no such address.

The Parks Department employee was first alerted to trouble when he heard gunfire, but even this sound did little to stimulate a near dormant curiosity imposed by his adolescent sangfroid. As shadows lengthened across the lake, however, he became alarmed that the canoe had not been returned and had gone to look for it. On the other side of a nearby peninsula that masked a view of a lovely cove, he found the canoe floating bottom upward with the paddle scraping against an outcrop of rock. There was no sign of the occupant, although he, by this time quite agitated, searched among the bushes and trees by the shore. Returning to the landing, he was about to report a possible drowning when Lieutenant McAllister arrived.

The police dragged the bottom of the lake for possible clues near the place where the canoe had been drifting. The rifle was found but no fingerprints could be retrieved, and the police speculated that the last user may have been wearing gloves. There were no more leads, despite intensive effort in the next few days, and then another event occurred that heightened speculation and sent the police in another direction.

Allison Fetherheft did not report for work, and after several days, as suspicion mounted among her subordinates that there might have been foul play, a warrant was obtained to search her house on the outskirts of town. Instead of finding a body, the police found – almost nothing. Sumptuous furniture, a mound of expensive clothes, and items of jewelry were there. But she was not.

There were, however, highly suspicious circumstances in a den with a door leading to her garage. Papers had been thrown about helter-skelter on the floor, and a chair and standing lamp had been overturned. The glass from the bulb of the lamp had shattered across the rug and parquet floor. A brown stain, subsequently identified as human O positive blood – the same blood type possessed by Ms. Fetherheft, according to her health records and a police laboratory report – was discovered near the upended chair. Flecks of dried blood led across the carpet and floor and through the doorway down a step into the garage. There they stopped. The car was gone.

Fetherheft had bulked large in campus life, and her departure was an electrifying development. When the news of the attempt on Ruth Dinsmore's life became public, as it was bound to after the local newspapers heard the story, the entire community was consumed with speculation. TV commentators gravely pronounced their views on the death of Kevin Pannelli and the attempt on Ruth's life. Now, as graduation neared, another mystery titillated both town and gown, and many on her cowed staff rejoiced at the prospect of Fetherheft's untimely demise.

However, Mrs. Ackerman was not one of them, as she hardly knew Allison Fetherheft except by reputation. On an afternoon filled with student appointments, she was seated at her desk before her computer, the guardian of the entrance to the dean's office. The door to the office was closed, for the dean had been closeted for over half an hour with his next-to-last visitor of the day. The time to commence the next appointment had come and gone, and still the door remained shut.

Mrs. Ackerman glanced with a perplexed frown at her wristwatch. There was still work to do, and she needed to give the dean the late afternoon mail and determine whether any matter of urgency should be attended to before going home. As graduation was now under two weeks away, there were many last minute details and problems that required attention.

But the door was closed. Idly, she picked up the stack of mail and sifted through it. One letter from a prospective student was labeled Personal and Confidential, and she held it to the light before opening it. Furtively, she scanned the contents. She next opened the remaining letters and folders containing interoffice memoranda, but there was nothing of particular interest except, perhaps, the note from the new student.

The school was quiet these days. The furor caused by the attack on Ruth and then the apparent abduction of Fetherheft had subsided. The time set aside for examinations had passed. Most faculty offices were empty, the occupants presumably at home grading examination papers. It was necessary for all grades of graduating students to be submitted at this time to the Registrar's Office to make sure that each student qualified for the degree. That office, as a result, was a maelstrom of frantic activity, the staff busily compiling lists and tabulating final grade point averages. But otherwise the halls were silent, the hubbub gone, save for the occasional, flickering ghost of a student come to check a bulletin board.

The door to the dean's office opened. The visitor was John Vandervoort, the student with whom the dean had spoken at the conclusion of the meeting of the Gay and Lesbian Law

Students Association. He and Dean Ansari were still engaged in conversation.

Holding the door, the dean was speaking. "I'm glad you came to see me, although I guess it wasn't easy. I'm not certain what I'm going to do. I'll have to think about it. But don't worry, your name will never be mentioned. I give you my word."

"I just don't want anybody to get hurt," John answered. "People have a right to privacy, but the reputation of the school is important, too."

The dean looked at him intently. "As I said, don't worry." He smiled. "Incidentally, it's been really nice knowing you these last three years. I won't have a proper chance to say goodbye at graduation. So I'll do it now. Good luck to you."

"Thanks, Dean. I appreciate it. And good luck to you. I'll bet running this place gets pretty heavy at times. Sorry to dump this one on you."

The two men shook hands. With a wave to Mrs. Ackerman, John walked by her desk and departed. The dean looked after him thoughtfully, a puckered frown on his features.

"Curious. Very curious," he said to no one in particular. Then, to Mrs. Ackerman: "Well, why don't you come in?"

Mrs. Ackerman rose wearily from her seat. When she entered the office, she found the dean standing by the window, his hands thrust into his pockets. He was looking out, and even after she sat down, he did not turn. A minute went by, then two, then three. Finally, with a shrug of his shoulders, he faced about and leaned back against the credenza standing next to the window. He folded his arms across his chest.

"God damn," he said. "If it's not one thing, it's another."

"It's about financial aid and Allison Fetherheft, isn't it," Mrs.

Ackerman said, her curiosity piqued. "I knew it. Didn't I say this whole mess was about financial aid?"

"Yes, you did, and I'm grateful for that. But Allison had nothing to do with the decisions about who would be a financial aid recipient. So it doesn't appear to involve me after all, or the other members of the committee – or I would have warned them. It seems she was right about that poem after all, although the sequence was out of order. She was the last one to die."

"How do you explain the attack on Ruth?" Mrs. Ackerman persisted.

"I... I can't. There's a lot about this whole damn situation that I can't explain, but I won't spend my life hiding in a hole wondering if I'm on the short list. I'm just glad Ruth didn't tell her folks and we'll see her at graduation."

"How do you know there won't be trouble at graduation?"

"Oh God! Put hiring extra police on the list of things to do... not that they seem to have the foggiest idea what's going on."

Mrs. Ackerman was still curious, and while it wasn't her place to quiz her superior, as the dean's confidante she had long ago assumed certain rights. "Well, if your conversation wasn't about Allison Fetherheft," she queried, "would you care to say what it was about? You seem upset."

"I'd like to discuss it, but I guess I shouldn't. Not now, anyway. I've got some thinking to do."

She inquired: "Is it something serious?"

"Yes. Well, yes and no. I mean, it could get us into trouble with the alumni, particularly the ones who give money." He paused. "On the other hand, people have a right to lead their own lives. God damn! I never would have thought it. Not in a thousand years."

Mrs. Ackerman folded her hands and looked at him sympathetically.

"What happened to the last appointment?" the dean asked.

"You mean Prigley?"

"Prigley Sassoon?" His question was unnecessary. There was no one else with that name.

"Yes."

"Oh dear. I guess we ran over quite a bit, didn't we. I forgot the time was passing. He didn't just get fed up and walk out, I hope. Anyway," the dean started to justify himself, "what we were talking about was important."

"Prigley said it was no problem," Mrs. Ackerman said soothingly. "It was about his graduation speech. He'll come back in a couple of days when he checks in with the Women's Association. He had to leave to do Ruth Dinsmore's laundry."

Mrs. Ackerman smiled. The dean looked at her incredulously. "Laundry? That wasn't part of the deal."

"Isn't that what got him into trouble in the first place?"

"Did he say Ruth's? He must have meant his own."

"No," Mrs. Ackerman continued to smile, "he very definitely said hers."

"I swear... that Ruth Dinsmore... she's nobody to run afoul of. I'll be damned." Reflecting, he also smiled. "Well, well, maybe we started something. Maybe there's more going on than meets the eye."

"I hope so," rejoined Mrs. Ackerman. "That would be wonderful."

They looked at each other. Mrs. Ackerman's eyes were twinkling. The dean shook his head. Unbeknownst to the other, both were wondering, as between Ruth and Prigley, which was the hunter, which the hunted. The moment passed.

Walking to his desk and, still ruminating, the dean sat down. He held out his hand. "What have you got there for me?"

"Just the usual, although you may be amused by the letter from that foreign student you admitted." Incautiously, she added: "I don't think the ending is very nice. That young man has a lot to learn. He must be just like his father."

The dean shot her a puzzled glance.

Did he suspect? Adding confusion to incaution, Mrs. Ackerman ventured defensively that she could not help noticing the last part of the letter when she opened the envelope. The dean accepted the explanation in amused silence. For a moment, as usual, he thought he had been at fault.

"Let's have a look at it. And you might as well hand me the rest. Oh, and there's nothing more today. Remember to call tomorrow and get extra police for graduation. Why don't you call it quits and go home?"

He pulled the letter from its envelope. Both were of flimsy paper, and he almost tore it in the process. The letter contained the following:

Your Excellency:

I was just thinking that I was becoming to the United States of America in April. But no! Now, however, I am arrived at your country, although I have been here only a short distance.

Through ministrations gracious and vivid from Mr. Frank Dinsmore business associate of my father, all problems of immigration were resolving with utmost dispatch.

Now I await exquisitely opportunity to meeting you.

It is a vast honor including me in your noble institution. Crabshaw School of the Law is being already, as you say in English, the apple of my eye.

To make a readiness, what I am doing? The question is of gravest importance. I fly to American Middle West states after two days. Are the accommodations to greet me? What kind of professor to whom I am having introductions? What kind of books and papers I am purchasing?

Other questions provoke me. Are you available? Is office of foreign students open, and is the president making herself available? Is it better to rent or buy a condom? I anticipate your answers with eagerness.

My father is sending greetings based upon your most warm welcome of him several months past when he is visited America.

With felicitations, dear Dean, I am saluting you with smacks of success.

Yours very truly,
Adamu Shoppa

P.S. My father inquires also to know if you are dismissing your secretary yet. A snitch in time saves nine, he says.

Halcyon Days in June

Chapter Twenty-Three

The Graduation

Graduation exercises of Crabshaw School of the Law were held in early June every year in a large, municipal auditorium. Neither the law school nor the university possessed a hall large enough to accommodate the members of the graduating class, their families and guests. So the auditorium, with a convenient parking facility across the street, had been selected many years before. Indeed, it had been used by so many graduating classes that, to use a time-honored legal phrase, the mind of man runneth not to the contrary. And, with the exception of a few doddering alumni, so it seemed.

The building had a distinguished air, as befitted the occasion. It had been built during the Great Depression as a public works project when labor was cheap. Solid columns with Corinthian capitals marched across the front, and the entrance was graced by a pediment with carved figures in bas relief of men and women engaged in various occupations. Most depicted manual labor on the farm or in the factory, but two were of a doctor wearing a stethoscope and a lawyer with outstretched arm and hand arguing a case. A person with a discerning eye and historic bent might detect that the homely face on the latter bore an uncanny resemblance to the incumbent mayor at the time of construction.

Inside, there had been equal attention to detail. The hall

was in the shape of a large semi-circle, lit by hanging lights in art deco style and reached through heavy, carved wooden doors at the head of each aisle. A stage jutted into the hall across the front in a smaller, parallel semicircle. Rows of chairs had been arranged on the platform for the faculty, distinguished guests, and members of the law school and university administrations. A box containing the certificates of graduation had been placed to one side, and a podium with a microphone stood in front of the chairs on the other side. Flowers had been arranged at the edge of the stage, and a banner hung from the podium.

The last was in purple – some thought garish purple – with white lettering that proclaimed CRABSHAW SCHOOL OF THE LAW. Underneath this title was the faint, discolored and barely discernible outline of other letters that had been removed. The banner had been sewn originally in the early seventies, and the additional letters had read LOVE IT OR LEAVE IT. Unfortunately, too many students had taken the hint; it therefore seemed appropriate to modify the original intent in favor of a more seemly, if bland, pronouncement.

Cars were pulling up to the front, disgorging passengers. Excited knots of people were ascending the front steps. Inside, on the floor below the auditorium, was a large room, the immediate objective of the arriving graduates. They were congregating there, in the midst of babble and hubbub, to put on their robes. Student marshals were attempting frantically to organize the happy throng into two long, snaking lines.

A smaller room was off to one side of this turmoil. In it, insulated from contact with the student virus, the faculty and members of the Board of Trustees were also robing. President Zo had arrived, filled with convivial cheer. The Distinguished

Speaker, who had been chatting with the dean, was struggling to adjust his mortar board. He was a local Superior Court judge who had conducted a vicious, law-and-order campaign to win office. A man of average height, slightly overweight, he had an unseemly wart that decorated the side of his broad nose. Some of the more radical students had objected strenuously to his selection as speaker, but President Zo had concluded that his notoriety would be good public relations for the law school and university. No one could have foreseen, of course, that within three years he would be indicted for taking a bribe. And to prove that trouble can come in pairs as well as threes, he was sued simultaneously for divorce by his wife for an adulterous liaison with his secretary. Their shenanigans were reported with barely muted glee in the press. But by that time, happily, his honorary degree from Crabshaw had been forgotten.

A student marshal, a yellow, plastic whistle dangling from a braided lanyard around his neck, appeared at the door and spoke to the dean, a note of urgency in his voice. "We have the students all lined up, Dean Ansari. Can we get the platform party ready? The music should start in a few minutes."

Almost all the faculty members had on their robes, a few bulking large in their new, bullet proof vests, and the few who did not rapidly donned them. With affable jostling, the faculty allowed themselves to be organized into two lines by the student marshal. The assistant dean scurried about officiously, a list in hand, making sure that everyone was stationed according to rank: the president, dean, guest speaker and chair of the Board of Trustees at the front followed by senior members of the faculty, then the junior members and, at the end, members of the Board of Trustees (usually the new ones, too inexperienced as yet to have concocted an excuse not to attend) and senior members of the administrative staff.

The last of the students were already departing their staging area, cheerfully marching in ragged order up the stairs to their final rite of passage. The platform party closed up behind them. There was a brief delay, then the lines moved forward again. The triumphal refrain of Elgar's Pomp and Circumstance drifted down the stairwell:

> *Land of hope and glory,*
> *Mother of the free,*
> *How shall we extol thee,*
> *Who art born of thee...*

"Hold up your robes – make sure you don't trip on them," someone shouted.

"I love that music," said the guest speaker, who was marching next to the dean. "What's the name of it?"

The dean turned to tell him. As he did, he took his eye off the stairs and trod directly on the hem of his robe while he was taking the next step upward. There was a tearing noise. In consternation, he looked down to see his robe flapping awkwardly from a long rip up the side.

He had been careful not to drink too much coffee, lest a call of nature trouble his role as master of ceremonies. He had fretted over various minor details such as the order of seating and his opening remarks. A torn robe he had never contemplated.

"Dammit!" The word was drawn out and uttered in emphatic frustration. The dean spoke to no one in particular. "I can't go on the stage like this. I'll have to get another robe."

The platform party came to a halt on the stairs. The last few students exited from the stairwell, proceeding in solemn order to their seats, there to stand respectfully as the platform party marched down the center aisle. The organist started Pomp and Circumstance for a third time. But the platform party did not appear.

The assistant dean thrust himself forward. "Dean, please hand me your robe. I'll get a new one for you, sir." He took the robe and elbowed his way in haste down the stairs, stepping on Boomer's foot in the process. Boomer bellowed his objection, and the raucous sound wafted into the auditorium.

In scarcely a minute, puffing, the assistant dean reappeared. "There are no more robes," he said with evident dismay.

"Why are we waiting here?" muttered a faculty member back in the line.

Junker turned and whispered irritably, "The dean ripped his robe." He rolled his eyes at the ceiling.

Land of Hope and Glory… was being played for the fourth time. The students, their families and guests continued to stand.

"Are there any safety pins?" President Zo inquired.

"I don't think so," the assistant dean replied.

The dean broke in. "How about just ordinary pins or a stapler – at the table where the students signed in." His voice had a frantic edge to it. "Go back, quickly, and see if you can find something."

Again the assistant dean descended the stairs. This time, however, he managed to avoid Boomer, who glared at him. Duxbury stood to one side, his face betraying amusement at the scene of ineptitude before him. It won't be long now, he thought, it won't be long before my crowd – and I – are running this law school. The clock ticked slowly – ever so slowly. Two, three, four minutes passed, then five. The assistant dean reappeared. Perspiration dotted his forehead. He was holding the dean's ripped robe.

"There weren't any pins, but I found some paper clips."

"Paper clips?" The dean had begun to wonder if someone else should take his place.

"Quickly," said the assistant dean. "Put the robe back on."

The dean obeyed. He had little alternative. Deftly, with President Zo and the guest speaker helping, the assistant dean fastened the torn edges together. Aside from an occasional, thin gleam of metal, the repair appeared to hold.

"All right," said President Zo with relief. "Let's get moving."

The lines started forward again. After the sixth refrain of Land of Hope and Glory, the organist had stopped. Most people continued to stand. Now, as the platform party appeared at the head of the aisle, the music welled up again. The audience turned, and the solemn procession filed between the ranks of graduating students. With dignity and decorum, their different colored hoods making them look like so many birds of brilliant plumage, the faculty marched to their seats on the stage.

The music stopped, and the dean stepped forward.

"Please be seated," he said into the microphone on the podium. His voice boomed out in the silence. With a rustling sigh, the entire assemblage sat down. The ceremony had begun.

As the dean returned to his seat in the front row, a rabbi, who had been seated at the end, walked to the podium to deliver the invocation. As Crabshaw was a private institution, unvexed by First Amendment concerns, every third year a

Protestant minister, a Catholic priest or a rabbi was asked to perform this job, and it was the rabbi's turn. God smiled upon Crabshaw. The prayer was brief, calling upon the Deity to bless the gathering which had been brought together in the joy of achievement, and to sanctify the tasks of those about to venture forth into the world. The law is a noble calling, the rabbi said, omitting to add that it can also be lucrative. His prayer ended in a burst of Hebrew. Most in the audience stared at him blankly. But if his words had been in Latin or, for that matter, English, their expressions no doubt would have been equally uncomprehending.

This formality dispensed with, the rabbi returned to his seat, and the dean rose and advanced to the podium. As he did so, a light bulb in a fixture in the rear of the hall ended its useful life with a loud, popping noise. Instantly, in a rattled response, the dean ducked into a crouching position behind the podium.

Aside from a small girl in a front row seat, the assemblage was silent, a few wondering if the ceremony was about to begin with street theater. Junker, seated on the stage behind the dean, his eyes fixated on the dean's posterior and the row of paper clips hemming his robe, once again rolled his eyes toward the ceiling.

"Look! Look, Mommy," the little girl chirped into the silence, "the funny man is hiding behind that wooden thing."

"Hush, child."

"Look, he's peeking out at us."

The dean had ventured a glance around the edge of the podium. He caught sight of a police officer in the rear of the auditorium waving frantically, in improvised sign language, that there was no danger. Slowly, he rose to his feet.

"Well, heh, heh," he faltered, "that was just a drill." The

assemblage stared at him blankly. "Just a little practice for the real thing… You know, the big one, heh, heh." A couple of members of the audience sidled down their rows and departed.

It was clearly time to salvage the meat of the program. Standing erect, without further elaboration on his inexplicable behavior, the dean delivered his opening, prepared remarks. He was followed by the chair of the Board of Trustees, who welcomed the parents and guests and congratulated the graduates. His comments were brief and poorly delivered. These shortcomings were more than made up, however, by the guest speaker whom the dean introduced next.

Perhaps he was not polished, and his thinking was far from an intellectual tour de force, but he had the rousing delivery of a district attorney which, in fact, he had once been. Bums and other assorted hangers-on of society were roundly excoriated. Vice received a verbal comeuppance. He praised family values, emphasizing that the civic virtues of loyalty, sobriety and self discipline begin at home. A few more people left the hall, and afterwards, some said his talk was more like a campaign speech than a commencement oration.

The moment of greatest significance, Conferring of Degrees, came next on the program. The dean walked to the podium and, speaking into the microphone, said: "Would the graduates please stand." They rose. President Zo stepped to his side. Turning to him, the dean continued: "President Zo, I have the honor to present to you the members of this year's graduating class."

Now it was the president's turn. Many of the graduates had given him no end of trouble, complaining about the lack of a cafeteria and inviting radical speakers to the campus. Rather spiritlessly, therefore, with a wry look on his face, he took the microphone and intoned: "Members of the graduating class! By virtue of the authority vested in me, I confer upon you the degree of Juris Doctor, with all the rights and privileges pertaining thereto."

Delirium followed. The graduates cheered, and a couple flung their mortar boards into the air. Family members and guests had risen, and there was a wave of clapping throughout the hall.

When the din subsided, Dean Ansari spoke again, advising the graduates to proceed, as directed, onto the stage. Each was to receive a certificate. The diplomas would be mailed in a month, for not all the final grades were tabulated, and a few of those receiving certificates would not finish their course work until the end of the summer.

It was therefore possible, under the circumstances, that not everyone receiving a certificate would graduate. Aware of this contingency, the dean had asked Mrs. Ackerman to prepare a certificate that would indicate that a diploma was forthcoming but not bind the school to furnish one. She had accepted the assignment cheerfully, sure of her command of the language. When the printed certificates were delivered a day before graduation, suitably inscrolled, each read:

> CRABSHAW SCHOOL OF THE LAW
> This Certificate Entitles You
> to a
> DIPLOMA
> Unless it does not

The dean was displeased. But it was too late to change the wording, and an admonition would have been fruitless.

Besides, Mrs. Ackerman would have made him feel like the transgressor. The certificates were duly handed to each graduate as he of she walked across the stage to shake the hand of the dean and the president. There was some tittering when they returned to their seats. Beaming with a sense of accomplishment and oblivious to the reaction, Mrs. Ackerman watched the proceedings from the rear of the hall.

This part of the ceremony took time. There were the usual antics: kissing the certificate and ignoring the president's outstretched hand seemed to be the most favored. Occasionally a father would push forward to take a photograph of a son or daughter descending the stairs from the stage. Finally, the last graduate returned to her seat to yet another round of applause.

By this time, however, the audience had begun to fidget. They endured the award of several prizes. Then, finally, at last, it was time for the farewell student address. The speaker was none other than Prigley Sassoon. The dean introduced him, and Prigley strode to the podium.

Most student speeches at the end of a commencement have a similar quality. They exhort; they condemn; they congratulate. Prigley's was no exception. His performance was no better or worse than most. Ruth listened to him in mixed admiration and agony. The difference came when he reached the end.

"This concludes the formal part of my speech," he said. "Now I would like to talk about something personal and then make an announcement of great interest to you all. So... here goes. First, the personal part. I'm not sure how to say this, so maybe the best thing to do is just go ahead and say it. I mean, so many of you are friends, and I want to share the news. Maybe some of you are aware that I only got to know our fellow classmate, Ruth Dinsmore, a few weeks ago. I mean, I knew her before then, but not really. Before then I didn't think we had anything in common, her being kind of an activist – sorry, Ruth, but it's true – and me, well, not an activist. At least, not that kind of activist."

There was laughter. Prigley was struggling. He had rehearsed, but his lines were forgotten. Ruth knew of the announcement of great interest, but she had had no inkling of the personal part. Now she suspected, and she started to redden.

"Anyway... " Prigley took a deep breath. "What I wanted to say is that Ruth and I are going to get married. We just decided this last week. Isn't that wonderful? Two things at once, sort of, I mean graduating and getting engaged to the most beautiful woman in the world."

He paused. Some people started clapping.

"Hey Ruth," he added. "Y'all come on up here. And bring your mother... I mean, I guess... my future mother-in-law." More laughter. "And, I forgot, our best man is going to be John Vandervoort. For you people here who don't know, he's another member of the class."

His remarks were clearly an impromptu part of the program. But it was a poignant moment for the graduates, and in any event Prigley had control of the podium and the microphone. Mrs. Dinsmore, trailed by a reluctant and embarrassed Ruth, walked up the stairs onto the stage and stood next to him. Smiling shyly, Ruth took Prigley's hand.

Mrs. Dinsmore was wearing a stylish, linen dress with a white carnation. A slightly plump, middle-aged woman, with light brown hair that had obviously undergone recent treatment in a beauty parlor, she looked out with bovine simplicity at the upturned faces before her.

Prigley began to speak again. "I'm not going to make the next announcement. I'm going to leave that to Mrs. Dinsmore. So this is her introduction. She has something important to say."

Unselfconsciously, he stepped back from the podium, still clasping Ruth's hand. Mrs. Dinsmore took his place before the microphone and unfolded some notes that she placed on the podium. Observing her, the dean was uncertain what to do. Unannounced and unscheduled speakers were not part of the program, but a potentially heavy-handed interruption would be awkward and might dampen the cheer of the occasion. He decided, for the moment, to pray for brevity.

"Thank you, Prigley. It's a great pleasure to be here for this wonderful celebration, and I would like to congratulate the graduates on their achievement."

Somewhat to the dean's surprise, Mrs. Dinsmore's speaking voice was firm although perhaps overly modulated.

"I do indeed have an announcement of importance to the school, and I'm only sorry my husband is not here. It should come from him, but regrettably he is away on business. He asked me to also convey his congratulations." She paused briefly, glancing from side to side. "My husband has a business partner in Africa whose name is Alhaji Baba Shoppa. Mr. Shoppa visited Crabshaw several months ago and spoke with Dean Ansari. He has a son, who, I understand, has been admitted recently to the school. Because of his fondness and respect for the institution, and for other, personal reasons, he has decided to make a gift to Crabshaw of twenty million dollars."

Until this moment the audience had been quiet, perhaps as puzzled as the dean by Mrs. Dinsmore's presence on the stage. At the abrupt mention of the donation, there was an audible gasp.

Mrs. Dinsmore continued. "Mr. Shoppa has asked my husband to establish the terms of the gift. While these have not been decided finally, and will be worked out in consultation with the dean, I can tell you that a significant portion of the money will go for scholarships and construction of a cafeteria. Another portion will be used to strengthen faculty compensation and the library. In addition," Mrs. Dinsmore turned to the dean, "Alhaji Baba Shoppa has expressed strong admiration for Dean Ansari and hopes he will oversee the expenditure of these funds."

Turning back to the audience, she concluded: "Thank you for allowing me to address you."

For a few seconds there was silence, then a thunderous wave of applause. A handful of faculty members, however, seemed unaccountably perfunctory in their enthusiasm.

The dean leaped to his feet, catching his robe on the arm of his chair. Paper clips sprayed across the stage. Undeterred, the rent robe flapping behind him, he moved toward the podium to acknowledge the gift and convey appreciation.

President Zo, however, was too quick for him. Brushing past the dean, he grasped the microphone. No longer did he need to stand, as it were, behind a curtain pulling levers. It was time for action. "By virtue of the authority vested in me," he blurted out, nearly smacking his lips, "we accept this splendid gift. We are deeply appreciative, deeply appreciative indeed. Dean Ansari, do you have anything you would like to say?"

Zo limped backward, his prosthesis landing directly on the fallen hem of the dean's robe as the dean stepped forward. The entire back of the robe ripped away. The dean looked behind himself in dismay.

"Only this," he said, clearly flustered. "We at Crabshaw will do our best to live up to this strong expression of support. Thank you... thank you very much." He stepped back, tripping over the large patch of black cloth that had been his robe and that had dropped onto the stage. After an ungainly pratfall, he staggered to his seat.

The ceremony was disintegrating. The rabbi had risen to give the benediction, but everyone ignored him. He stood in the middle of the stage, his fine prayer unrecited. A marshall had begun to organize the platform party into two lines to depart, but the dean had forgotten to announce that the audience should remain seated. People began to rise and mill about.

The dean found himself standing next to Mrs. Dinsmore. The Marshall had asked her to join the recessional procession.

"Where are you from?" she whispered.

"What?"

"Where are you from?"

"Oh. You mean originally? Connecticut." He had not realized this was a social occasion.

"I love the East Coast," she burbled. "Whereabouts in Connecticut?"

"I grew up in Waterford."

"Waterford! We have the most wonderful, close friends in Waterford! Frank and I met them a couple of years ago when we were in the Bahamas. Have you ever been to the Bahamas?"

"No." The dean was having trouble hearing her. The organist had begun to play the recessional, and the line was moving slowly toward the stairs leading from the stage.

"Well…" Mrs. Dinsmore was speaking breathlessly. "The Bahamas are simply beautiful. But I was wondering if you know the Petersons. Ned and Alice Peterson. They live on Green Street."

"I haven't lived in Waterford for many years. I don't even know that street." It probably isn't in the part of town I grew up in, he thought.

"You don't know the Petersons? I thought everyone in Waterford knew them." Mrs. Dinsmore was no longer listening to the dean's replies. They were irrelevant. "Ned is a broker. He sells stocks. He and Alice have the most lovely family. I think all the children are in good schools. And, I must say, they live in the most *beautiful* home. It's on a hill. Frank and I visited them there once, and they were so kind to us. They asked over lots of their friends. You must know them…"

By this time, the procession had proceeded up the aisle through a gathering, jostling crowd of graduates and guests. Mrs. Dinsmore was still talking as the sedate column rounded the corner at the end of the aisle to return downstairs.

Chapter Twenty-Four

A Final Communication

My dear Dean Ansari, the letter began, easily betraying – if flimsy paper and a foreign stamp were not indications enough – that it was from a foreign source. Scanning the return address on the envelope, the dean could see immediately that it was from Alhaji Baba Shoppa. In bold type, the words Personal and Confidential had been written below the dean's name as addressee. That alone would have piqued his curiosity, particularly from the father of an incoming student and, in addition, the school's most generous – indeed, lavish – financial benefactor. Perhaps a further gift was in the offing.

The letter began with an explanation that it had been composed with the aid of a translator who worked at the British Embassy and who had been, for an unspecified gratuity, sworn to secrecy. Dean Ansari read it rapidly but carefully, his lips pursing and his brow knotting as he progressed. When he finished, still holding the letter in his hand, he swiveled around in his chair and stared for several minutes out the window. Then, rotating his chair to its previous position, he read the letter again, then laid the sheets carefully on his desk, folded his hands in his lap, and sat in brooding, quiet contemplation.

The letter was an astonishing document. *With considerable difficulty*, it said, *I write to explain events at Crabshaw School of the Law during the past year*. It continued:

Shortly before your graduation exercises at Crabshaw, I was visited by my American business associate, Frank Dinsmore. He came here to discuss a new venture in the United States. Unfortunately, when he arrived at my residence, I was not at home, and he was greeted by my new wife, a woman known to you as Allison Fetherheft. Mr. Dinsmore recognized her immediately, having met her on a previous occasion, and they engaged in conversation. Upon returning, I realized that our little deception was at an end.

I have known Allison (I call her Allie) for many years, and we have – how shall I say? – been involved romantically for a long time. Whenever I journeyed to the United States, which was often, I would endeavor to see her. Ideas of beauty differ. In your country, emaciated women are apparently in vogue, whereas in my village, where I grew up, a woman's attractiveness is proportional to her poundage. I was immediately, and, may I say, irrevocably drawn to Allie's delicious heft. Her bulk is the delight of my eye.

Over time, however, I began to notice that the furnishings in her house were increasingly opulent. The reason was unknown to me. I suspected an inheritance. It was not until after she arrived in my country, and we wed, that I discovered the true state of affairs. Of course I forgive my Darling for her unfortunate indiscretions. I am grateful, too, that the lack of an extradition treaty with the United States will permit her to live securely with me for the remainder of our lives. We are delightfully happy, even if the servants do seem a trifle nervous in her presence.

It appears that Allie was borrowing money from the financial aid account of your law school to pay for her life style. I dislike the word embezzlement. She meant to return the funds, although at the time she was unable to do so, and now, of course, we have – through me – made restitution in full.

Regrettably, however, before she could rectify her paltry pilferage, a nosy student assistant in the university's Accounting Office became – as you say in the States – wise to her game. His name was Thomas Headly, and he confronted her twice in her office. The second time there was an infelicitous altercation that became loud enough to attract attention. Allie begged him to be quiet, and finally he agreed to meet with her privately that evening on the top deck of a nearby, multi-level parking garage.

There the argument continued. He threatened to expose her and rather unwisely revealed that he had, that very evening, slipped a memorandum detailing his suspicions under the door of the chair of your Financial Aid Committee – your colleague (whose name escapes me) who is reputedly jolly and of pumpkinesque appearance. I am sorry to say that, because of Thomas' rude, accusatory and contumacious behavior, my Darling became justifiably enraged and pushed him over the edge. To avoid detection, she disposed of his body on the pavement under a window of his apartment building, correctly and luckily guessing that the window was his.

Following this regrettable incident, my Darling contacted one of her subordinates – a feral character named Charlie Traynor. My Sweet obtained his eager compliance when she hinted that, without his cooperation, she might be forced to reveal sordid details about his past. Because of his official duties, this man had access to all offices and an intimate knowledge of the building. He promptly secured the memorandum – which, I regret to say, he then had the foolish temerity to read – but the clumsy oaf revealed his whereabouts when his carnal urges overwhelmed his need for secrecy and discretion. Allie was distraught when she learned how badly he had frightened the young woman who discovered him, but at least by then he had nearly completed his assignment.

As bad luck would have it, Thomas had spoken before his death to another law student, one Kevin Pannelli, about his suspicions. He gave Kevin copies of some of his purloined papers. But because of Thomas Headly's tragic and untimely demise, Mr. Pannelli had to proceed on his own. My Sweet became aware of his activities – indeed, hot on the scent, he came to her office making foolish inquiries – and she correctly divined his underhanded intentions. That was the very day that I visited you. Shortly before the conclusion of their unfortunate meeting in her office, obnoxiously waiving the papers at her, he informed her that he was returning to the law school and was going to speak with your Financial Aid Committee about further investigations.

She realized that he would go first to his locker in the basement of the law school to obtain his books. Allie was to meet me at approximately the same time, so she fetched her automobile and drove to a parking lot behind the law school, where we had a delicious moment of

221

reunion. As a simple and natural precaution, she usually carried a claw hammer in her handbag. After asking me to wait momentarily while she transacted some business, my Darling entered the school through a side door. At the time I knew nothing, I assure you, but I now understand that she surmised that this Mr. Pannelli would visit a bathroom before going upstairs, and she therefore waited for him in a nearby storeroom. Her intelligence, her stunning foresight, came into play!

Before retrieving his books from his locker, Mr. Pannelli advanced to the men's room. He had, apparently, purchased some sort of doll as a present for his boyfriend, and he was holding it under his arm. There was a confrontation. When my Pet demanded the sheets of paper in his hand, Mr. Pannelli refused to relinquish them, saying in a most haughty and supercilious tone that he intended to go to the police. My dear Allie was forced, under the circumstances, to strike him rather smartly about the ears with her hammer. She then relieved him of the papers, tucking them in her purse.

The doll had fallen to the floor, and she picked it up and placed it on the seat in one of the booths. Then, in a brilliant stroke of deception designed to confuse the authorities about the nature of his untimely demise, she took down his pants (naturally, averting her eyes) and removed her rather old shoes, placing them before the doll on the floor. Creeping stealthily past the janitor's office in her bare feet, she returned to our automobile, never uttering a word of complaint about the cold to her delicate toes. I was, naturally, somewhat taken aback by the speed of our departure, but I attributed it to her natural delicacy in not wishing to be seen in any kind of compromising situation with a person of the opposite sex.

Having discovered how easy it was to enter locked offices of the law school at night by using his master key, I'm afraid Mr. Traynor resumed his career as a petty thief by breaking into them to steal petty cash and other minor items of value. His activities went unreported, the unlucky victims apparently attributing their losses to error or inadvertent carelessness. One evening, however, his nasty disposition and lust betrayed him. The already confusing state of affairs at Crabshaw was muddied further when he viciously raped Janet Harbrough, a member of your administrative staff. Needless to say, my Allie became alarmed at the reckless indiscretions of her subordinate and admonished him to terminate his naughty behavior.

And so here matters might have rested, had it not been for your own investigations and, if I may be permitted to say so, your ill-advised decision to ask Ms. Ruth Dinsmore to assist you in snooping about to discover what had happened to your financial aid funds. Alas, my Darling knew nothing of Ms. Dinsmore's background or of my business association with her father, but she did soon perceive that Ms. Dinsmore was walking, so to speak, down the same path trod by the late Messrs. Headly and Pannelli. The researches of Ms. Dinsmore became more persistent, and a silly poem, composed and then pasted carefully by Allie on the president's door, did nothing to throw her or you off the track.

Corrective action became necessary, and my dear Allie, her heart nearly broken with grief at the thought that yet another student would have to be administered a painful object lesson, concocted a clever disguise and, one afternoon, followed Ms. Dinsmore and a bumptious student lothario to a nearby reservoir. Modesty compels me not to allude to the purpose of their tryst. My Pet's plans went awry, and I believe there is no need for me to acquaint you with the details of her botched effort. Sufficient to say that, to use one of your American barbarisms, you happened upon her get away, wig askew, and my Sweet incorrectly concluded that she had been discovered at last. The jig, so to speak, was up.

Returning home, Allie collected money that she had hidden, and in her haste to depart she knocked over a lamp, cutting herself in the process. Again, her formidable intelligence came into play! She realized that her hasty departure could be made to look like an abduction, and so she contrived to set the scene. I shall not bore you with the details of her further flight, some of which are confidential and involve persons who would not wish their identities to be revealed, but I will say that considerable sums of money have a way of easing the difficulties of travel and immigration.

Before quitting the country, however, one untidy detail remained. Allie realized that she needed to chat with Charlie Traynor. That unreliable and, I must say, foolish man had learned too much. Knowing his whereabouts, she sought him out. Unfortunately, instead of agreeing to her justifiable and entirely reasonable demands, he thought to negotiate an inordinate sum in return for his silence about the memorandum from Thomas Headly to your rotund professor. My Pet took umbrage at his cheeky behavior. There is no need to relate the disagreeable and rather messy details. I'll say merely that she was the last person to see him alive.

When Frank Dinsmore spoke with my darling wife, I was stung by the realization that her presence here, once known, would result in pesky questions, investigations and, ultimately, the revelation of the truth. And you can imagine, my dear Dean, my intense mortification when I grasped that my cherished business partner might discover that my wife had attempted the murder of his daughter! How else is one to say it? I thought: was there a way to make amends, and the answer came in a brilliant flash. In gratitude for the admission of my son, but in fact as an act of penance, I could make a gift to your esteemed institution.

This I have done. Moreover, should my imbecilic son actually persevere to graduation, I hope that my business affairs – until now so graced by the benevolent eye of God – will permit me to make an equal or greater donation.

With this expectation in mind, I write to you, necessarily telling all so that you can effectively neutralize any comments or inquiries that my partner might make. As Allie is safely beyond the reach of U.S. law, and as you never offered aid or assistance, there is no way that your complicity can make you an accessory after the fact. And Crabshaw, I assure you, will benefit handsomely if my business affairs in your country can progress unhindered by any hint of scandal. I am presuming, therefore, that we share a mutuality of interest, and that I can rely upon you to maintain my revelations in confidence, terminate your further inquiries into the missing financial aid funds, and deflect intrusive questions by over-zealous police regarding recent events at your school and the whereabouts of my darling wife.

And so, my dear Dean, I trust that old, unhappy chapters are behind us, and that we can look forward to a new chapter – to, as you say, a clean slate.

With every good wish for the continued prosperity of Crabshaw School of the Law, and with my most earnest and cordial sentiments, I am,

Sincerely yours,
Bobby (Alhaji Baba Shoppa)

P.S. Have you dismissed your secretary yet?
P.P.S. Now that you have read this letter, please burn it.

Summertime

Chapter Twenty-Five

Bathroom Bob Sounds a Sour Note

Mattress Head was seated in the dean's office, his long legs stretched out in front of him. In the gathering heat of a summer day, his unkempt mop of hair was no advantage. Otherwise, his appearance was appropriate to the season, his sense of taste and the absence of the student body. Wearing sandals, shorts and a loose fitting T-shirt, emblazoned with the words "Mean People Suck" across the front, he seemed relaxed except for the frequent, vehement jabs with his forefinger that punctuated the conversation.

Graduation had taken place six weeks before. The procession had descended without mishap to the robing room. Mrs. Dinsmore, babbling the entire time, remembered the names of the guests at the party in Waterford and described them in luxuriant, painful detail. Near the end of her monologue, balancing duty against a desire to flee, the dean had wondered whether it might be possible to walk in a somnambulistic trance. He was spared by the boisterous arrival of Ruth and Prigley, who soon disengaged Mrs. Dinsmore in order to attend the reception that followed the graduation ceremony.

After Mattress Head had entered the dean's office and seated himself, he first inquired how the police investigation was proceeding. The dean had hesitated before answering, "I spoke recently with Lieutenant McCallister. He said that they'd run into a dead end. No more clues to chase. They're keeping the case files open in case further information is forthcoming, but for now the active investigation is closed."

"There are no leads at all?" Mattress Head inquired earnestly.

The dean squirmed uncomfortably in his chair. "None, I'm sorry to say. McCallister has an idea but not enough evidence. He thinks the culprit is Charlie Traynor – you know, our former janitor. He had a motive to kill Kevin."

"But what about Thomas Headly?"

"Thomas Headly was a good student," the dean said, a sad caste to his face. "What a waste. And you're right, no motive there that we know of, which does weaken the case against Charlie. On the other hand, the rape case is pretty strong. Charlie had a key to all the offices, he wears the same kind of shoes as the rapist, and whoever did it was wearing a mask, which suggests he knew he could be easily identified."

Mattress Head looked puzzled. "Um, sure, I guess," he faltered, "but wasn't he... you know... kind of gay. That's the rumor, anyway."

"Well... I'm no psychologist, but maybe he did it because he's bisexual or he hates women. That strikes me as a possibility, and I know from personal experience that he had a lot of anger in him." Rubbing his chin, the dean shifted his gaze momentarily. "As you may know, the police questioned him at length and couldn't pin anything on him. And now he's vanished."

"If it was him," Mattress Head said, "he'll do it again somewhere, and when he does, the cops may get him. These guys usually slip up sooner or later... but, I hate to say it, the sexual assault may just be one of those crimes that never gets solved." He paused for a moment. "What ever happened to that nice young woman, Janet, who was the victim of the rape? I haven't seen her around lately."

In a subdued voice, the dean answered: "Poor kid. She went back to New Mexico, where she's from. Broke up with her boyfriend, I heard. When they commit these crimes, these bastards never think about all the collateral damage they also cause to family and friends. Not... I guess... that they give a damn." He shrugged and, in an effort to appear nonchalant, added, "For now... for now I think we can be thankful that everything's been quiet for several weeks, and personally I don't believe there'll be further trouble."

"Good to hear it," Mattress Head said. "Anyway, Dean, that's not the main reason I came here." He then reported a recent escapade involving Boomer and Duxbury. Unasked, that duo had decided that the faculty lounge needed an upright piano. To be more specific, Duxbury had decided to donate his battered piano to the school and take a large charitable deduction on his tax return. No matter that the lounge abutted most faculty offices and the faculty library and that faculty members frequently sat in the library's deep, imitation-leather chairs to contemplate and read.

With fanfare and laughter, they had dragged Duxbury's unsolicited gift down the hallway and maneuvered it against the wall of the lounge. Mattress Head, who had been in his office reading, was rudely interrupted. To make matters worse, the following day in mid-afternoon Boomer decided to knock out a few pieces of early jazz. Even if he had been proficient, which he was not, the noise would have been disruptive. The cacophony drove Mattress Head home with a severe headache.

"And as if that wasn't bad enough," he complained to the dean, "I had a run-in with Bob just a few minutes ago."

"Oh? Really? What happened?"

There was nothing unusual about a run-in with Bathroom Bob. Apparently this one had been out of the ordinary.

"I came in about an hour ago. And I had a cup of coffee and read a newspaper. And after I glanced at the newspaper, I started to read some serious stuff. And then, a few minutes later, I heard singing. Like someone was trying to imitate Caruso or Pavarotti or something."

"Singing?"

"Yeah, singing. Really loud. So, okay, I thought it would stop, but it didn't. I couldn't work. So I put the article down – the one I was trying to read – and I went out into the hall. And it was pretty easy to tell that the sound was coming from Bob's office."

The dean looked at him quizzically. "Go on," he said.

"So I knocked on his door and walked into his office. He was just standing there, singing at the wall. I said something… like, I don't know, maybe, 'Hey, people are trying to work around here. Will you knock it off!' And he stopped and gave me this funny look and said, 'What's the matter with you?' For God's sake, can you believe it; he asked, what's the matter with me?"

Mattress Head was getting excited, and his voice rose.

"So," he continued, "I said something like 'Why are you singing?' And he said, 'Because I haven't sung in a long time.' As if that answered the question! I told him to quiet down. Actually, not just quiet down. I asked him to knock it off, because I was trying to work, and I may have shouted a little. Then he said, 'Why are you complaining? We've got a new piano now. I heard someone playing it yesterday. This is just a delayed sing-a-long!' And then he told me to get out – get out of his office. And when I just stood there... I mean, I was speechless... he crooked his head to one side... you know the way he does... and pushed me and slammed the door on my finger." Mattress Head held up a red finger.

Speechless in turn, the dean gaped at the finger. Slouched in one of the chairs near the low coffee table on the opposite side of the couch from Mattress Head, he rose and walked to the telephone on the rear corner of his desk and dialed Bathroom Bob.

"Hello, Bob? Massoud here," he said icily when Bathroom Bob picked up the receiver. "I have no doubt you know why I'm calling. Would you mind telling me what's going on? This is an academic institution, not a place to audition for the opera."

Bathroom Bob answered defensively that, yes, he had been humming somewhat loudly. Many people, he said, like his humming and think he does it very well. He didn't realize, in the summer, that anyone else would be in so early.

"Did you check?" the dean retorted. "And humming isn't the way I heard it. Anyway, what about pushing a faculty colleague out the door and slamming it on his finger?"

"I did not slam it on his finger," Bathroom Bob answered, again rather defensively. "He was very rude to me. Very impolite. When he left, I shut the door firmly, and just as I did, he put his finger in it."

The dean sighed. "I think you and I had better have a chat. And I think an apology is in order. In the meantime... I don't care about the piano... which I never heard about until ten minutes ago... no more singing."

Replacing the telephone in its cradle with a sharp click, he looked at Mattress Head and shook his head. "You were right to see me. We'll get this cleared up. You're entitled to peace and quiet, and I think you're due an apology."

Mattress Head had been agitated when he arrived, knocking abruptly on the dean's door. Now he looked relieved. "Okay. Good. Okay," he said. " I didn't realize you didn't know about the piano."

"No, I didn't. We'll have to do something about that, too. People can't be playing it when others are trying to work."

Mattress Head rose to depart. As he did, the dean remembered that there was something else he wanted to say. "Can you wait a minute," he asked. "While I've got you here, this is a good time to find out if you to can do something important for the school."

Stopping at the door, Mattress Head turned around.

"We have a new foreign student," the dean continued, "and it's critically important that he pass his courses and graduates. He needs a tutor, and you're a good person for the job. He doesn't write English very well."

Mattress Head was prepared to feel sympathy toward an entire continent, but he was repelled by the thought of helping an individual student.

"Well, okay." He did not want to appear negative. "But, you know, I have a lot of research to do. And I'm not sure I can teach grammar and composition and things like that. What about someone else?" He tried desperately to fob off the task. "Others really write better than me, and they're not so busy."

"This is the son of the man who gave us all the money."

"Really?" Why had not the dean said so in the first place? An important person and an important assignment! Brightening, Mattress Head visualized lavish dinners, at which he would be the sole guest, and sumptuous gifts from a grateful, admiring and, most important, rich student. Perhaps he was not as busy as he had imagined.

"On second thought," he said, hastily reversing himself, "I guess I'm the best person for the job. Of course I'll need to brush up on English composition, but you know I'm always willing to take on extra duties for the school."

For a moment, the dean surveyed Mattress Head with curiosity, trying to divine his motive. "Good, and thanks," he said finally, giving up the effort. "You can start when the next semester begins. Now I think I'd better walk downstairs with you and take a look at that piano."

Chapter Twenty-Six

A Final Revelation

They started off down the hall, Mattress Head walking with stork-like, jerky strides next to the dean. Not having anything further to discuss, each was silent. At the end of the hall, the stairway led to the faculty offices, the mailroom and a lounge on the floor below. The dean had thrust his hands into his pockets. Observing him deep in thought, Mattress Head discretely held open the door at the foot of the stairs. With patently manufactured cheerfulness, he then said goodbye and returned to his office.

The dean ambled down a corridor to the faculty lounge. A secretary, fluttering by with a sheaf of papers, noted his abstract expression and his failure to voice a customary greeting. As he was about to turn the door handle, he glanced sideways. Junker and Duxbury were entering the hallway together at the far end. A frown creased his features. Instead of pausing to say hello, which he might have done earlier in the year, he pushed the door open and walked inside. No one was there.

He poured himself a cup of coffee and surveyed the offending piano. It looked innocuous enough, dilapidated but sturdy, save for its incongruous placement in the faculty lounge of a law school. Absentmindedly, the dean noted the key-hole in the cover to the keyboard so that it would be possible to lock the instrument against use except on those rare occasions when there might be a party in the lounge.

Another reason for unpopularity, he thought. There will have to be rules about when the piano can be used. He walked to the open window, coffee cup in hand. I'm not so certain, he mused, whether Alhaji Baba Shoppa did me a favor. Am I obligated to stay and oversee the use of the money? This is a free country, isn't it? Dammit, why did Mrs. Dinsmore make his sentiments known in public? It would be awkward to refuse, yet it feels as much like a sentence as a reprieve.

He stared moodily at the bright green leaves on a tree outside the window. Another thought was plucking at his consciousness. He had caught a glimpse of Junker entering the hallway. The dean had a chore to perform. He had delayed. In fact, he had delayed too long, and now was as good a time as any to do it.

Still holding his cup of coffee, he quit the lounge and walked to Junker's office. The door was closed, and he knocked. A gruff voice bade him enter.

* * * * *

When Junker and Duxbury had arrived shortly before, they had been animatedly discussing the scope of and limitations on the application of the 11th Amendment to the United States Constitution. It is a complex and confusing area of the law. Junker thought 11th Amendment doctrine might apply to a problem he was trying to resolve, and he had solicited Duxbury's advice. Regrettably, Duxbury knew little about the subject and was of limited assistance. Both had caught sight of the dean but gave his presence little thought.

However, when Duxbury reached his office and placed his pearl handled umbrella in his umbrella stand, the image of the dean recurred to him. He removed his jacket and shoes; it was going to be a warm day. Pensively, he slumped into the leather chair before his desk. Then he leaned forward, placing an elbow on the desk and his bearded chin in his hand. With his other hand he picked up a pencil and tapped it on the desk's cluttered surface. For several minutes he sat motionless except for the slowly tapping pencil, staring vacantly at the disordered piles of books and papers before him.

At last he stirred. Whatever his thoughts may have been, Duxbury seemed to arrive at a solution. With a faint smile, he swung his chair around, stood up, and padded in threadbare socks to a bookcase. There on a shelf about half way up from the floor, next to a thick volume on the Law of Partnerships, stood the clay figurine.

Duxbury's bony hand closed around the little, brown figure. Fondly, he gazed at it for a few moments, then returned to his chair. The small figure he placed carefully, almost reverently, on his desk. Again he seemed to lapse into distracted thought, but only briefly. With a determined, deliberate movement, Duxbury grasped the small statue and turned it this way and that, holding it for a minute against the light streaming through the window. His expression was of utmost concentration. Apparently satisfied, he rose again, returned to the bookcase, and placed the figurine in a dark cave behind a volume on a lower shelf. It vanished, hidden from view, once again his private totem of conflict with masked and buried parts of himself.

This scene was acted without a sound. His sigh was audible, therefore, and jarring in the silence, when, seated before his desk for the third time, he picked up a student paper and began to read.

* * * * *

Junker was also reading when the dean accepted his invitation to enter. He had a text on constitutional law before him and was leafing through the index to determine whether the book might contain an answer to his question. When he saw the dean, his face registered surprise. Dean Ansari rarely visited his office, and he quickly tried to surmise what might be the reason for the visit.

"Come in, come in," Junker said. His manner was neither cordial nor rude. "You can take those books off that chair and put them on the floor." He waived in the direction of a semi-upholstered chair before his desk. "Please sit down."

The dean did as he was bidden. He had not smiled and, like Junker, his expression was business-like and serious. Before the dean could begin speaking, Junker inquired, "To what do I owe this visit?" There was a hint of warmth – or was it mockery? – in his voice. Not pausing for a response, he added, "Actually, I've been expecting you or, at any rate, wondering whether you would want to talk with me. Ever since the meeting."

The dean furrowed his brow, looking slightly perplexed.

"You know," Junker continued, "the meeting of the faculty several weeks ago. The one we had over at the university." He shot the dean a piercing glance. "I spoke against you. I am sorry that was necessary, but I felt the occasion demanded a candid assessment."

The dean had not come to Junker's office to talk about the meeting, and he was thrown off by the way Junker had quickly seized the initiative in the conversation. Rather than interrupt, it seemed best to let this topic run its course.

"No problem. Of course," he murmured, searching his

mind to recall what Junker had said, "everyone had to be forthright. I tried to be forthright, too."

"And you were."

"Until I was interrupted."

"Yes." For the first time, Junker smiled. "What did you expect from a law faculty?"

"That committee... the one the president appointed... it never met, as far as I know, and I don't think we'll ever hear from it."

"So much the better." The words were harsh. Junker's brusque manner had returned. "Anyway, as long as we're being straight with each other, I want you to know that I regretted the public nature of my remarks. But not their content. I oppose you, and to be perfectly frank, I shall continue to oppose you."

The two men looked at each other, each gaze level and unblinking.

"Perhaps," the dean said slowly. "Perhaps not. Actually, I came here to talk with you about something else." His tone was even, unruffled. For some, unaccountable reason, he felt a surge of confidence.

Junker arched an eyebrow. "What do you have in mind?"

"Well," the dean said, "I want to talk with you about something that's highly personal. Personal, that is, to you. Unfortunately, it can also involve the school, or I would never bring it up."

Did Junker shift imperceptibly in his seat? His intent stare never left the dean's face.

"Have you ever heard of The Lace and Leather Lounge? It's sometimes called, by those in the know, The Triple L Ranch, or so I'm told. Over in Middleford?" He asked the question directly and without emotion.

This time Junker did shift noticeably in his seat. "Yes," he said, "I've heard of it."

"Have you ever been there?"

"Why... do you ask?" Junker's cheek twitched slightly.

"Well, as I said," the dean answered, "I wouldn't bring this up, but if the reputation of the school is jeopardized, in particular our ability to raise money from our alumni, then I really have to. I've got to find out what happened, and I must demand that it stop, if it's true.

To come to the point," he cleared his throat, "one of our students came to see me several weeks ago. He was with a couple of friends, and he told me that he saw you... in The Lace and Leather Lounge. In fact, on the stage. You were dressed up in women's clothing... rather scanty clothing... with high heels, mesh stockings, lipstick and a wig. And you were dancing. I'm told it was a rather suggestive dance."

The tips on both sides of Junker's mustache rose at the same time.

"And is there any reason why they should have thought it was me?" There was a tremor in Junker's voice, but his manner was cold, even hostile.

"Unfortunately, yes. The person on stage was quite distinctive, due to his mustache. It could not be hidden. So, later in the evening, my informant went outside, in the rear of the building. He stood in the dark by a shed. He saw you come out a back door, dressed, I guess, somewhat the way you are now. He saw you get into a car. He took down the license plate number, and it happens to be the number on your car." The dean stopped talking.

Junker sagged in his chair, and his intent stare wavered. He placed his palms over his eyes and sat motionless in that posture for several moments. Then, dropping his arms, he rose convulsively and walked to the window behind him. But in a second he spun around, agitated, and took two paces back into the room. Placing his hands on the back of his chair, he stood facing the dean. It was as if he were using the chair as a barrier for protection. His eyes were fixated, protruding in fear.

"For goodness sake, sit down." The dean's voice was quiet, almost sympathetic. "This doesn't have to go any further than the two of us, and the student told me he would not discuss it. Figure it out for yourself. He's got only slightly less interest than you in admitting to anyone that he was there."

Junker's body deflated in a long exhalation of air. Slowly, his eyes still on the dean, he resumed his seated position.

"So, I suppose it's unnecessary to ask," the dean said, "but I'm going to ask anyway. Is it true?"

The words seemed caught, fluttering, in a sticky web of air, as if they never reached Junker. Unhurried, the dean waited in patient silence until, finally, in a voice barely audible, Junker said, "Okay." Not yes; not no. But the admission was enough.

"Then," the dean continued firmly, but without condemnation, "let me say this. Your feelings are your own business, and so is your private behavior. However," and he emphasized the word, "I must have your promise that this sort of public exhibition will never be repeated."

Once again, in a whispered tone of limp resignation, Junker answered, "Okay."

The dean stood up to leave. Head bowed, Junker remained immobile, staring at his hands that were folded on the desk in front of him.

"Assuming we get along in the future," the dean concluded, couching his words carefully, "and there's no reason why we shouldn't, you have my word that I shall tell no one."

Junker nodded in dull affirmation. He had caught the hint of veiled blackmail, and he acceded to it.

Dean Ansari had no reason to pity his adversary. And yet he did, and he barely restrained the impulse to reach out with a reassuring hand. For a few moments he stood, gazing at Junker's drooping head. Then he turned quietly and departed, closing the door gently behind him.

* * * * *

For a long time, perhaps half an hour, Junker sat nearly motionless. He folded and unfolded his hands. Occasionally he closed his eyes. Finally, rousing himself, he pushed his chair back from the desk. The bargain was sealed. His livelihood depended on the dean's assurance. Adjusting his tie, he rose stiffly, hesitated, then strode from his office.

Duxbury was still engrossed in the student paper when Junker walked in.

"Hello," he said. "I was just thinking of you. Come over for some coffee?"

"No." Junker's voice was husky.

"Are you all right?"

"Yes."

"Are you sure? You look like you've just seen a ghost."

Junker smiled wryly. "The ghost of my past, perhaps... or maybe the ghost of what I ate for breakfast."

"Well, brace up, my good fellow. All's right with the world."

"I am perfectly braced up, thank you very much."

Duxbury was startled by the abruptness of the response. He shot Junker a questioning glance.

"You haven't called a meeting," Junker continued, shifting the conversation to the reason for his visit.

"A meeting? What meeting?"

"You know, the one we were going to have after graduation to talk about Badger – I mean, the dean – and what further action we might take."

"Oh, *that* meeting," Duxbury responded genially. "We're not going to have it. For one thing, the others have left on vacation. They must have forgotten. Anyway, our game was over when that potentate gave us all that money. Surely that must have occurred to you."

"Of course." Junker was not going to take lessons in mental acuity from Duxbury. Besides, he had personal, private reasons for surrender. "Zo will never relinquish his support of the dean now."

"Would you, if you were in his shoes with the possibility of so much money?"

"No, I guess not. But that means," Junker said, almost wistfully, "that means it's over. We might as well face up to it. We've lost."

"Lost? Well, I suppose we have. But look at it this way. We may be stuck with the dean, but while we're at it, we're all going to be a lot richer."

Duxbury smiled.

Epilogue

Duxbury smiled. God laughed. Actually, it was not so much laughter as a long, low chuckle, a cosmic murmur of amusement. The foibles of God's human creatures are a never-ending diversion and delight. Often their foolishness involves sexual shenanigans, but it can take any form. The antics at Crabshaw were a particular case in point.

So God looked down from heaven, and He laughed. He? Ruth Dinsmore would have something to say about that. And rightly so. The Deity hardly needs sexual organs to create, or if God does, then our Creator is most probably a hermaphrodite. The notion of an anthropomorphic God, however, implies that God is as screwed up as we are. That is an unseemly suggestion. Let us settle for neutral nomenclature like God or Deity and leave the flowing white hair and woolly whiskers to the imaginings of prior generations.

If we do that, though, we are going to have to abandon the notion of looking down from heaven. The All-Seeing need not look, and heaven is unlikely to be a place tucked conveniently behind some far-flung galactic cloud. Perhaps it would be better to say, then, that all creation – every chain of amino acid, every atom buried in each burning star – shook with silent mirth. The universe, unlike Queen Victoria, was amused.

And the best is yet to come. The dinosaurs, after all, were not very funny. They were, in fact, a monstrous, dreary, reptilian food chain lasting millions of years. Human beings, of more recent vintage, are a different matter. They provide genuine amusement. But they are only a way station in a relentless march from bug to Boomer to something beyond. Looked at another way, they are a point in an evolutionary process from somber silence to muted merriment to boisterous hilarity. Eons hence, the universe will not merely chuckle. It will regard itself amidst gales of scarcely controllable, joyful laughter.